Beyond the Waterfall

by Marnie L. Pehrson

First Edition 2005

Published by CES BUSINESS CONSULTANTS

Cover photo from Microsoft ClipArt Gallery Online

www.MarniePehrson.com
www.CleanRomanceClub.com

Printed in the United States of America

ISBN: 0-9729750-7-1

Chapter One

Jillian couldn't see a thing. The blindfold wrapped so securely about her eyes that not even the rays from the warm afternoon sun could penetrate the woven material. The obstruction of vision heightened her awareness of the sounds and aromas emanating from the rushing river rapids. Her cousin, Running Deer's strong hand gripped her upper right arm while the tall, strapping Chief Joseph Vann escorted her on her left. Carefully they guided her over the rocky terrain.

"Watch your step here, Jillian; it's a little difficult," Running Deer warned as he helped ease her over a large stone.

"Wait right here," the Cherokee Chief's deep voice commanded authoritatively, but not harshly.

Jillian stood perfectly still atop the boulder. She felt one muscular arm encircle her back and the other slip behind her legs. Weightlessness followed. She knew it was Chief Vann who carried her. He was married and seventeen years her senior, but still the thought of having this handsome, powerful leader lift and carry her to their final destination sent a surge of excitement through her twenty-year-old heart.

Jillian felt a cool spray cast moist droplets against her skin and heard the rushing of great waters as the temperature dropped cooler instantly. She drank the musky dampness into her lungs, and her nose twitched from the pungent heaviness. She could hear the Chief's boots sloshing through liquid. He exerted no more effort in transporting her across the cave than he would in moving a kitten from one side of a barn to the other. Besides the musty odor of their surroundings, she knew they were in a cave because she could hear the men's voices reverberating against the cavern walls.

The sloshing sound ceased, and she suspected the men had stepped onto solid ground. Chief Vann carefully set her feet to the cave floor, and her cousin removed the blindfold from her eyes.

Jillian gasped at the spectacle before her. Four torches lined the walls - two directly in front of her, one to her left and another to her right. The flames flickered and danced, sparkling against an entire cavern full of shimmering gold and silver! Large gold bars blanketed the cavern floor, and gold and silver coins heaped over and spilled from baskets placed haphazardly around the cave. The light refracting off the precious metals gave the entire cavern a luminous orange glow.

In wonderment, Jillian stepped forward and then stopped, turning toward the chief and pointing to a basket of gold coins, "May I?"

He nodded affirmatively, and Jillian squatted down, inserted her hand into the coins, letting them trickle through her slender fingers and clink back into the basket.

One remained in her palm. Examining its Cherokee markings on either side, she watched the dazzling light from the torches bounce off the shiny surface.

"It's beautiful," she noted and then gently replaced the coin. "Is all of this yours?"

"Some of it," the chief nodded. He wore a tailored suit, his dark thick hair cropped short, and his kind twinkling brown eyes smiled at her. He was six foot six and an amazing specimen of a man. Refined, educated and kind, he'd risen far above his father, Chief James Vann, who before him had become a hardened drunk whom many feared but few loved.

"Most of it is the Cherokee nation's," he continued.

"Remarkable," she whispered in awe.

"There are more treasure repositories like this one," Running Deer commented. "All hidden. Only a privileged few have seen them."

"That is why you blindfolded me?" she asked.

"It is safer for you this way. You'll not be able to tell anyone how to find it."

Joe Vann reached over and lifted six shiny silver pieces from a basket at his feet. He handed them to Jillian, "Purchase what you need for the village with this."

She nodded with understanding and slipped the silver into a leather pouch.

"We must always use silver when bartering with the white man," Joe Vann explained. "Gold sets their lustful hearts ablaze. They already suspect the wealth of our lands and are doing all within their power to dispossess us."

Joe Vann lifted the blindfold, and she turned her back to him so that he could place it over her eyes.

Soon she was traveling back downstream, winding through the rapids on a canoe. When they had gone a sufficient distance and hit calmer open waters, Running Deer removed her blindfold. She squinted, allowing her eyes to adjust to the intense brightness of the afternoon sun. Once she could see clearly again, she noted the trading post ahead, nestled among the orange, red, and yellow foliage of autumn. Smoke billowed from the chimneys, rising and hanging suspended like a child unwilling to drift too far from her mother's apron strings.

Jillian's task lay ahead of her - trading for the items her village needed. She'd been sent by her father and the other members of the council because of her unique skills. She had learned English from her parents who were both half-white, had learned to read from the Moravian missionary school at Spring Place and learned the art of trading from her father. Joseph Vann, also known as "Rich Joe," was the second wealthiest man in the United States and served as Chief of the Eastern Cherokee Council. She felt honored to travel in his company and pondered on the ramifications of what he had told her earlier in the cave. What would become of her people should they be driven from their lands?

Jillian stepped off the canoe onto the grassy embankment. Joe Vann and Running Deer accompanied her on either side as they ascended the hill toward the trading post.

"I have a matter of business at the livery," Joe Vann motioned toward his left. "I shall meet you here when I am done."

Running Deer and Jillian nodded and turned toward the mercantile. Three intoxicated, burly mountain men lounged like fattened hounds after a heavy meal. Their loud laughter and howling conversation echoed forth from the porch of the log building.

Jillian kept her eyes fixed on the doorway and told herself to proceed onward as if the ruffians were not there. Running Deer put his hand on his cousin's arm, offering her the security of his presence. He was a tall young man with thick dark hair and penetrating brown eyes. He did appear older than his seventeen years, but still, he would be no match for these vagrants should they decide to become violent.

One of the men whistled loudly while the other two made insinuative remarks about her beauty and her ability to bear a man handsome sons. Anger rose in a red heat on Running Deer's face. His fists clenched and the muscles in his bare arm flexed. She recognized trouble ahead with only a glance in her cousin's direction and put her hand over his fist.

"Never mind them," she whispered in Cherokee, and the pair continued forward and stepped onto the wooden porch. The boards creaked with the men's weight as they rose from their languid positions. Just as Jillian and her cousin were about to enter the building, one of the large men, with mud splattered across his shirt and a reeking stench of rum on his unattractive person, stepped over, obstructing the entrance.

"If you will excuse us, please, sir," Jillian countered coolly in clear and perfect English.

The man did not budge, and Running Deer glanced quickly over his shoulder to see if he could spot Joe Vann, but their leader was nowhere in sight.

"And what have we here?" the inebriated miscreant pointed to the leather pouch around Jillian's neck. His speech slurred so incoherently that Running Deer couldn't understand the man's English, but he could guess what he wanted by the way the reprobate eyed his cousin and her purse of silver.

"Please allow us to pass, sir. We have business inside," Jillian answered unflinchingly.

"Perhaps you should make your transactions with me, young lady. I can give ye what ye need," the man grabbed Jillian's chin, sliding his filthy paws along her face and toward her neck. Reflexively she held her breath. Running Deer attempted to pull the man off his cousin, but he may as well have been a fly trying to move a mule.

"Get Joe Vann," Jillian urged Running Deer in their native tongue, and Running Deer bolted down the porch steps toward the livery.

"Your young man is a coward," the man's intolerable breath suffocated her, and Jillian coughed from the stench. Just as the man would have dragged her off to an ignominious encounter, his body jerked away from her like a mangy mutt hauled by the scruff of its neck.

"Leave the young lady be, Chet," a tall, brown-headed white man ordered. While her attacker was more flab than sinew, her rescuer was nothing but brawny muscle. He stood taller than the drunkard, and transporting him by his grimy shirt collar, shoved the mongrel aside onto a rocking chair. The cur's weight fell backwards, and he flipped the chair over, landing on his flabby backside. His companions did not come to his aid, but rather burst into intoxicated laughter.

The handsome man, who looked to be about Jillian's age, gazed at her for a moment, his emerald green eyes engaging her cinnamon ones.

"Have you been harmed, Miss?" he asked as his penetrating gaze moved from her face down the length of her.

"No, sir," she shook her head negatively, and the man's observation returned to her face, noting the softness of her features. While from her skin tone, long dark hair and high cheekbones, he deduced that Cherokee blood ran through her veins, there was a soft European quality to her gentle features and full lips. A most exquisite combination, he thought.

"I am terribly sorry for your trouble, Miss." He extended his hand to her, "I am Jesse Whitmore. I would be more than happy to help you with your purchases."

"Thank you, sir," she nodded, and he allowed her to enter the building first. After she'd stepped inside, Jesse redirected his gaze, giving the drunken mongrel the stern expression a canine owner would issue a disobedient pet. Turning his attention back to Jillian, his features softened as he solicitously accompanied her through the store. She selected bolts of fabric, needles, thread, quilts and other assorted items.

Suddenly Running Deer and Joe Vann stormed into the mercantile, surveyed the establishment and marched straight to Jillian's side.

"Have you been harmed?" Joe Vann asked with concern as Running Deer put his hand gently on his cousin's back.

"I am well. This gentleman helped me," Jillian pointed to Jesse. She noted the clear admiration on Jesse Whitmore's countenance as his eyes lifted toward the six-foot-six Cherokee Chief's face.

"It is a pleasure to see you again, Chief," Jesse stated with marked respect in his voice as he extended his hand.

"You as well, Mr. Whitmore," he answered, giving Jesse a hearty handshake. "Thank you for looking after Jillian."

"A pleasure, Sir," he smiled.

Joe Vann turned to Jillian, "It appears as if you are in Mr. Whitmore's capable hands. I have a few more items of business, and I shall return shortly." He paused, reached into his vest and pulled out a piece of silver and handed it to her, "Select something for yourself while you are here."

"Yes, Sir. Thank you, Sir," she nodded and smiled gratefully.

"Running Deer, come with me. I need your assistance," Joe Vann instructed, and the two men departed.

"Is that your husband?" Jesse inquired.

"No," Jillian chuckled lightly. "I am not married."

"I see," he nodded, and his eyes smiled at her, but his lips did not. How did he do that? She wondered how his eyes could relate kind happiness without actually betraying the emotion in the upturn of his lips. Her eyes fell to those lips momentarily. They were full, and he wore a mustache with no beard on his strong square jaw. There was a slight cleft in his chin. She did not allow her eyes to linger on his face, although she would have gladly let them remain if she could have done so without his awareness.

He continued to help her gather the items she needed, and she had quite a stack on the mercantile counter by the time she handed him the six silver pieces. Then, Jesse reminded her that Joe Vann had given her some silver to buy something for herself.

"May I make a suggestion?" he asked.

She followed him to the counter. He stepped behind it and retrieved an ornate silver comb that a woman would wear in her hair. He set it on a black velvet surface in front of her.

"Only hair as lovely as yours would be a fitting residence for this fine a workmanship," he flattered.

She could see him mentally pulling her hair back and affixing the comb in her locks. She diverted her eyes from his and studied the comb, pretending that she was attempting to ascertain its construction. A nervous flutter came over her. She did not know what to do with such a sensation for she had never before experienced anything like it. Even being carried by Joe Vann could not compare with it. The encounter with Vann was more like the excitement one would feel in the presence of one's hero. This was different - much different!

"This looks too expensive for only one piece of silver," she noted.

"Yes, I suppose it is, but perhaps you have something else to add to the exchange?"

"It's extraordinarily beautiful, but I have nothing else to offer," she laid the comb gingerly on the soft velvet.

"I will let you have it for the silver and a picnic lunch," Jesse offered in his best bargaining voice, turning sideways to rest his elbow on the counter in front of him.

"A picnic lunch?" her eyes darted up to meet the mirthful twinkle in his.

"Saturday at noon. If you'll prepare a picnic lunch and spend the afternoon in my company, you may have the comb."

Jillian's heart fluttered even more furiously than it had before. It would be a shrewd bargain on her part. One piece of silver, a picnic lunch and an afternoon with this handsome man in exchange for a beautifully fashioned silver hair comb was an advantageous trade on her part. But she didn't even know this man. Yet, he did rescue her from the ruffians, and Joe Vann felt her safe in his care.

Jesse could tell the beautiful young woman weighed her decision carefully. But he also knew by the look in her eyes upon first seeing the comb that she wanted it. As a matter of fact, it was almost the exact expression she'd given him the first time his eyes held hers. But how badly did she want the comb? Badly enough to spend an afternoon with a man she didn't know? He found himself holding his breath, anticipating her reply.

"You drive an... interesting... bargain, sir," she drummed her fingers on the wooden surface. Then coming to a decision, she slid the silver toward him and took the comb.

"Where" she asked, trying not to meet his gaze directly. His eyes were smiling again. His lips were parted slightly, but still the corners remained unchanged. She shook her head nervously, a bit tongue-tied. And Jillian was never tongue-tied when bargaining. That's why she'd been selected to trade for the village.

"Where do you wish your picnic, sir?" she finally managed.

"Do you live in Spring Place?" he asked, deducing that she probably lived in Joe Vann's community.

"Yes," she answered.

"I will meet you at the village entrance at noon," he instructed as if he were simply arranging for the delivery of merchandise at a specific time and location.

"Very well, noon Saturday it shall be," she nodded affirmatively, extending her hand to him in agreement. He took it in his grip, and a thrilling hammering resounded throughout her body as he held it lingeringly in his. The couple's eyes and hands were still locked when Joe Vann and Running Deer entered the mercantile and joined her at the counter. Self consciously, Jillian retrieved her hand.

Joe Vann noticed the large quantity of goods that Jillian had acquired with the silver. With one raised eyebrow he watched her slip the silver comb into her leather pouch. Mr. Whitmore thanked them for their business, and the three left with Jillian's purchases.

As they loaded the merchandise into their two canoes, Joe Vann commented, "The village is fortunate to have you as their trade representative."

"Why is that?" she asked.

"In all the time I've been trading here, I have never seen the mercantile come out on the short end of an exchange, but today you have come away with more than you bartered."

She did not wish to explain anything, but he looked as if he wanted clarification. And when Joe Vann wanted an explanation, an explanation he received.

"There were some intangibles involved in the transaction," she could feel the blush rise to her cheeks, and she cast her gaze downriver instead of at the formidable leader.

"Intangibles?" Running Deer's voice held a tinge of alarm as his worried gaze darted toward Joe Vann. What had his cousin bartered?

"What kind of intangibles?" Joe Vann prodded.

"A picnic lunch with the new owner of the mercantile," she muttered, hoping they wouldn't hear what she said nor ask her to repeat herself.

Joe Vann's hearty laughter rang out across the water. When his humor subsided, he elbowed Running Deer, "This Mr. Whitmore is a shrewder trader than I gave him credit for."

Her cousin nodded with a knowing smile. It took every ounce of self-restraint Jillian could muster to keep from throwing one of those bartered blankets over her head to hide her embarrassment.

Chapter Two

Jillian checked her basket one last time: venison, fry bread, corn-on-the-cob and grape dumplings. She placed a blanket over the basket and bid her mother farewell.

Sophia Elliott had never seen her daughter so nervous. Jillian was a headstrong young woman who never let things rattle her, but it was obvious that the mercantile owner had gotten under her skin. Her hands trembled, and she'd fidgeted with that picnic basket at least a dozen times. Jillian's father, John Elliott, had even taken the opportunity to visit Joe Vann to find out what he knew about the young man.

The Chief had been impressed with Jesse and suggested he encourage the relationship between his daughter and the mercantile owner. "Our time is passing, old friend," he said. "A marriage between Jillian and Mr. Whitmore would give her the security and protection of marriage to a white man. It may even be sufficient to protect you and your family in the days ahead."

John Elliott had taken the Chief's advice under serious consideration and assisted his daughter by hunting for the deer and helping her prepare it for her bartered meal.

Jillian stepped out of the house and strolled down the road to the village entrance with her basket hanging on her forearm. Many yards before she reached her destination, she spotted Jesse with his white shirt, suspenders, black pants and shiny boots. His arm leaned nonchalantly atop a fence post. His posture straightened slightly as he caught sight of her approaching in a beautiful blue dress, her hair pulled back in the silver comb, just the way he'd imagined it that day in the store.

As she drew closer, he walked toward her, greeted her and took the basket, shifting it under his right arm and extending his left to Jillian. She put her hand on his arm as they made the brief trip to his wagon. Jesse put the basket in the back and assisted her in climbing into the front.

"It sure smells delicious," he commented.

"Thank you," she accepted the compliment graciously.

"And your hair looks lovely," he noted.

"Thank you," she blushed.

"Of course, I knew it would," he smiled.

"You did, did you?" she chuckled softly.

"That's right," he nodded. "It's my job to know exactly what the customer desires, and then make certain she has the opportunity of acquiring it."

"What gave you the idea that I desired this comb?" she asked. She knew she was a savvy trader, and she didn't think she'd betrayed her overt interest in the piece.

"It was not the comb to which I referred."

She looked at him quizzically. If it wasn't the comb he knew she wanted, then what was it?

"Think on it a spell, Miss Elliott," he winked, and then his countenance transformed into the most endearing expression she'd ever seen on a man's face. His green eyes twinkled, and a smile that made him look even younger, spread across his handsome face. He cracked the reins, and the team trotted along down the road.

Suddenly Jillian realized the insinuative nature of his remark. Her mouth dropped in astonishment, and her eyes darted toward him and then away as crimson flushed her cheeks. How presumptuous! She thought. Then again, it would not have been presumptuous on his part if her fervent interest in the man were as transparent as she feared. She simply must attempt to contain her emotions where this man was concerned! It was as if her entire soul lay bare before him like a gold ring shimmering inside a glass box.

"Where are we going?" she finally choked out in an attempt to alleviate the awkward silence.

"Somewhere I've never taken anyone before," he answered.

They rode for some time making casual conversation, discussing their families. She learned that Jesse was third oldest of eight children while Jillian was the third eldest of six. He'd purchased the trading post only a few months earlier from his uncle, having been raised by a store owner himself. From his accounts, she deduced that he was quite the enterprising young man, although he did not brag in the least.

After traveling for some time, Jesse finally stopped the wagon along the river underneath the sprawling red leaves of a maple tree. He helped her descend and led her through the woods. The further they walked, the louder the roar of the rushing waters. Finally, as they emerged into a clearing, Jillian beheld the most exquisitely crystal clear blue lake fed from the opposite end by a flowing waterfall.

"It's lovely," Jillian gasped in wonder that she had never seen this place before, yet oddly enough, something about it seemed familiar. She thought perhaps she'd been there as a child and simply couldn't remember. They found a clearing, and Jesse laid out a blanket on the grass alongside the lake and motioned for her to be seated.

Jillian spread out the meal before them, and Jesse ate heartily and complimented her culinary skills. She wasn't sure what to expect from the man. She'd heard tales of white men who took advantage of native maidens, but Jesse was a perfect gentleman. He asked thoughtful questions and listened attentively as she told about her life in the village. He was fascinated by the Cherokee lifestyle, their advanced civilization and obvious wisdom. He'd always admired their respect for women - especially their custom of placing women in their leadership councils.

Jesse gazed across the lake at two ducks that had settled into the water. After a moment of silence, his expression grew more somber, "I fear for your people, Miss Elliott."

She watched him and waited for him to continue.

"There are those who want your lands so badly, they would think nothing of driving you out and stealing it for themselves. Ever since a young Cherokee lad bartered with a man up in Tennessee with a gold nugget, they've been convinced that your people hide treasures of gold on your lands."

Jillian's pulse quickened as her mind flashed back to the treasure cave that Joe Vann had revealed to her only a few days prior. The sound of the rushing waters from the falls made the memory even more vivid, and her eyes darted across the lake. A waterfall! Could this be the very spot? Surely not!

"They'll stop at nothing, I fear," Jesse concluded, noting the apprehension on Jillian's face. "Are you well?" he asked.

Her eyes turned from the waterfall back to Jesse, "Joe Vann fears the white man shall dispossess us of our lands. If they do, where shall we go?"

"I've heard that they want to drive the Cherokee west," Jesse flung a rock, and it skipped across the lake, jumping seven times.

"How did you do that?" she asked, hoping to change the subject to something less foreboding.

"You need a good flat rock," he stood and stepped closer to the bank, picked up a handful of stones and returned to Jillian. Outstretching his hand, he helped her rise and selecting two stones, handed them to her.

"It's in the angle and the wrist," he demonstrated again by skipping another rock counting eight jumps. Jillian tried to mimic his movement and threw a rock, but it only skipped once.

"That's good for a first try," he encouraged. "Try again." She tried another, but the second one only plunged into the water. She shook her head in frustration and then bent down to find another rock.

"Here, take this one," he handed a smooth flat stone to her and demonstrated once more how to sail the rock across the surface of the water. The next time she tried, it skipped three times, and he jovially congratulated her and encouraged her to keep trying. Jillian's determined efforts to master the skill kept them both skipping rocks for nearly an hour as they talked, laughed, and enjoyed the autumn afternoon and the cool breeze that blew from the falls.

Finally Jesse looked up at the sun's position, noting several hours had passed since they'd left the village. "I should take you back. I have work at the store."

Jillian hated the afternoon to end. She had enjoyed his company so much, but she nodded understandingly and helped him gather up the blanket and the basket. When they arrived back at the village, Jesse helped her descend from the wagon, thanked her for the delicious lunch and the enjoyable afternoon, and bowed gallantly to kiss her hand farewell.

She wistfully watched him ride away, folded her arms about her waist, and pulled her shawl snug around her shoulders. The late afternoon air had grown chilly, but Jillian didn't mind. Her thoughts were of Mr. Whitmore and the afternoon she'd spent in his company. She wondered if she'd have the privilege again. Neither of them had mentioned anything about a future meeting, and she anxiously looked forward to her next trip to the trading post for a chance to see him again.

Fall turned to winter, and the days grew shorter and frigid. One early December morning, Running Deer came to Jillian's home to escort her to the trading post to barter for supplies. It had been nearly three months since she'd last seen Jesse Whitmore, and she wondered whether he would be at the post. She selected her best dress and wrapped herself in warm furs. When she saw Running Deer arrive, she kissed her father and mother and bid her younger siblings farewell. Her cousin extracted his hand from beneath the warm furs he'd wrapped around himself, and tugged her atop his black and white paint.

They rode for some time and then stopped by the river and climbed aboard a canoe. He blindfolded her and took the canoe downriver. After traveling for some time, the roaring of the rushing waters increased and Running Deer stopped the canoe.

"Stay here, and I'll get the silver," he tied the canoe to a tree, and Jillian could feel the boat tip as Running Deer stepped out. An unsettling feeling swept over her, and she simply had to know. The sound and the sensation of the cool breeze and mist spraying against her skin were all too familiar. She waited for several minutes, and then when she felt Running Deer would be out of sight, curiosity got the better of her and her thumb gently lifted the folds of cloth, and she peeked beneath them. The canoe floated at the edge of the lake, and a waterfall plunged its icy contents into the crystal clear blue reservoir. She knew the place well, and as she looked across the lake to the embankment, she pictured herself and Jesse skipping rocks across the placid surface on a colorful autumn afternoon. Little had she or Jesse known how close they were to a Cherokee treasure as they spoke of it that afternoon nearly three months earlier!

Jillian heard footsteps and quickly replaced the blindfold, pulled her furs tighter around her body and folded her arms so that her hands buried within the warmth of the pelts. She felt the boat tip from Running Deer's weight joining her. He untied the boat and rowed back into the river. After traveling for some time, he allowed Jillian to remove her blindfold as they approached the trading post. Upon this visit the trees were bare and covered with frost. Smoke billowed from the chimneys of the buildings, further fueling the misty grayness of the winter sky. Frosty mist hung in the air as Jillian exhaled into her hands to warm them. Running Deer helped her from the canoe, and she pulled the fur tightly around her. He handed her several pieces of silver, and she placed them into her leather purse.

Fortunately, due to the frigid morning, no ruffians loitered outside the mercantile. Running Deer and Jillian stepped into the toasty blanket of Mr. Whitmore's establishment. A fire blazed in the fireplace, and a potbelly stove in the corner of the spacious building provided further heat. Jillian's eyes traveled the room starting at the wall covered with quilts and skins, around to the coats and dresses and to her left. Her heart seemed to accelerate as her eyes searched and finally rested on the counter behind which she hoped to find Mr. Whitmore. It wasn't the handsome merchant she found there though, but another older gentleman with a gray beard and mustache. She recognized him as the former owner and exhaled deeply as her heart sank. Disheartened, she stepped toward the wall of quilts and resigned herself to the fact that she would not be seeing Mr. Whitmore on this visit.

Running Deer went in the opposite direction in search of blades and whetstones. As Jillian reached up to examine the handiwork on a wedding ring quilt, she heard the deep intonation of his voice.

"Good morning, Miss Elliott. What may I help you find today?"

She felt the smile spread across her face, causing her cheekbones to rise even higher. She forced the smile from her lips in an effort not to appear overly eager.

"Good morning, Sir," she greeted without removing her eyes from the quilt before her. She dared not turn about for she knew her countenance would certainly betray her delight in seeing him once more. He stepped closer to her, and she could feel the heat emanating from his body behind her. As the wind howled outside, her eyes darted toward the door that stood open. Snow had started falling and swirled into the store. She felt like melting into the warmth of him as his hands took her shoulders comfortingly, and the elderly gentleman at the counter hurried to secure the door.

"May I assist you in locating something in particular?" he spoke softly into her hair and continued to keep his hands snug on her shoulders. The presence of his powerful hands on her person sent tingling warmth throughout her entire being. She wondered if he knew that the only thing in particular for which she searched that day was him. At least he was the only thing she could remember that she wanted to find. After a few moments of dizzying distraction she remembered her list, pulled it from her leather pouch and handed it to him.

"Please, these are the items we require," she said.

His hand encompassed hers as he reached for the list. She could feel the heat rise to her cheeks, and her heart leapt to her throat as his fingers lingered upon hers. Nervously she lowered her hand and thrust it inside the folds of fur.

She closed her eyes, took a deep breath and then turned to face him. His green eyes smiled into hers, and she wondered at how he could make her feel so completely befuddled with only a twinkle in his eye.

"It is a pleasure to see you again, Miss Elliott," he nodded.

"And you as well, Mr. Whitmore," she inclined her head graciously.

"Let's see here," he directed his attention to the list and began gathering items and placing them on the counter while Jillian selected the quilts that appealed to her.

Occasionally, her eyes darted secretly toward him and then back to the quilts. Her mind was not on the acquisition of blankets; it was completely engrossed in the attractive mercantile owner. He looked so handsome in his winter wool suit and his leather boots. He'd grown a beard to keep him warm for the winter, and she thought it made him look even more manly and distinguished. As he returned to her side to discuss an item on the list, her mind set to wondering upon whether his beard would be course or soft to the touch.

When Running Deer had to repeat a question, his eyebrows furrowed. It wasn't like Jillian to be so distracted. Running Deer couldn't understand their conversation because he stood at a distance, and his English wasn't that good, but what they said was unimportant. Jillian's body language spoke volumes. Her complexion had a rosy glow, and her eyes gazed expectantly into the tall mercantile owner's. The merchant's hand leaned against the log wall behind Jillian, and he held up a fabric as if he were discussing its suitability, but his eyes were drinking from Jillian's lips.

A smirk crept over Running Deer's face, and he chuckled softly to himself. He expected Jillian would come away from this exchange with an excellent passel of goods for their village. He just hoped his cousin would be wise in her bartering of intangibles. Running Deer didn't completely trust any white man. Traders in particular gave him cause to beware for if anyone knew the secrets of what you owned, it was they.

"How did you travel here," Jesse asked across the counter from Jillian.

"By canoe," she answered.

"Only one canoe?"

"Yes," she replied.

"It's too great a parcel of merchandise you have here for only a single canoe. Why don't I deliver it for you? I'll bring it out this afternoon," he offered.

"It would be too much to ask, too great an inconvenience on your part," she gestured negatively.

"Not if you're willing to pay a small delivery fee," he offered knowing full well that Jillian had spent the last of her silver on the supplies.

She turned to her cousin and back to Jesse, "We'll just do our best to load it into the canoe."

"Aren't you going to ask what the delivery fee is, Miss Elliott?" he prodded.

"I haven't any more silver, Mr. Whitmore," she shrugged as if the price were irrelevant.

"Silver is not what I desire," he replied, leaning his elbows on the counter and gazing into her eyes.

She swallowed nervously, "What then?"

He leaned across the counter and whispered into her ear, "A stroll with you." The warmth of his breath on her neck sent a shiver over her as goose bumps rose to her flesh.

She hesitated momentarily and diverted her gaze away from him, continuing in her most businesslike tone, "Perhaps it would be wise to have you deliver the goods. We wouldn't want any of them to fall into the water on the way home, would we, Running Deer?" she turned her gaze to her cousin.

Running Deer's eyes darted to the merchant suspiciously and then back to her, "No, I suppose not."

"I'll bring it by this afternoon then," Jesse's eyes twinkled with his engaging smile.

Running Deer and Jillian took a few of the most pressing items with them to the canoe and left the rest for

Mr. Whitmore to deliver. Once they'd climbed into the canoe and Jillian had bundled several quilts around her legs and lap, Running Deer rowed the canoe out into the river. A few snow flurries danced around them, but did not settle.

"You fancy the merchant," he stated coolly.

"You know not of what you speak," Jillian rolled her eyes.

"You're an awful liar, Jillian. You shouldn't attempt it."

"I lie not," she defended.

"Then you are fooling yourself," Running Deer raised an eyebrow as his oars rhythmically caressed the water.

"He is rather handsome," she mused aloud.

"You best mind your back, Jillian. White men cannot be trusted. They always want something - whether it be our lands, our treasure or our women," Running Deer's face grew stern.

"He seems harmless enough to me."

"That's because you've your head floating amongst the clouds. Mark my words, that man wants something. You can see it in the way he stares at you." Running Deer's expression lightened suddenly and a teasing twinkle illuminated his dark brown eyes, "Then again, perhaps he's simply in love."

~*~

Jesse's uncle Welt leaned his gray head across the counter and winked at his nephew, "So have you talked that pretty maid into showing you to Vann's treasure trove yet?"

Jesse's eyes darted around the store ensuring that no customers were present to hear his uncle's brazen remark.

"I'm certain she has no idea where it is, Uncle," Jesse continued straightening a pile of quilts.

"Ah, who are you foolin'? I know what you're up to. Every time that girl comes in here, she's got a purse full o' silver and half the time she's on Rich Joe's arm. She knows, Jesse. She knows where that treasure trove is, and if you charm her right, she'll lead ya straight to it. I just hope you'll remember your old uncle here when you're richer than Midas."

"You're an old fool, Welt."

"I may be old, but I'm no fool!" he pointed his finger at Jesse knowingly.

Chapter Three

Running Deer pulled the canoe ashore, stored it beneath the undergrowth, and they loaded the provisions atop his horse that was still tied to a tree alongside the river. With the horse loaded, there was only enough room for Jillian so Running Deer walked alongside as she rode. The sky had turned an ominous gray, and the clouds clearly spoke of snow. As the pair entered the village, they were met by a loud commotion. It seemed nearly everyone in the village had gathered about and were busily discussing something of great excitement.

Anxious expressions and tear-stained cheeks owned the villagers' faces. Jillian hopped down from the horse, and Running Deer caught the arm of a young brave.

"What has happened?" he inquired.

"It's Chief Vann. They are driving him from his home," the boy answered with great remorse.

"Why? How can they do that? Who has done this?" Running Deer continued to hold the boy by the arm.

"It's the state. They've sent men to drive him off his lands. They came last night and threw a burning log upon the floating staircase to smoke them out. Then they came in brandishing rifles, shooting up the place. They saw that the fire was put out quick enough. They aim to steal his house of course. They've ordered him to have his family out by tomorrow morning."

"Was anyone harmed?" Jillian's eyes brimmed with tears.

"Just a boarder staying in the guestroom. He got shot, but wasn't killed," the lad answered.

"Will he leave or stay and fight?" Running Deer clenched his fist, ready to take on the entire United States military if need be.

"What right do they have to do this thing?" Jillian's angry eyes darted from Running Deer to the young man.

"The Chief intends to leave. He says fighting will just make things worse for the rest of us. They say he has broken a law."

"What law?" the cousins inquired simultaneously.

"I do not know," the boy shrugged his shoulders.

"May I borrow your horse?" Running Deer asked the lad. The boy willingly handed him the reins. Running Deer turned to Jillian. "Take my horse and deliver the provisions. I'll go find out what is happening and help Joe Vann gather his belongings."

Jillian nodded with understanding and watched as her cousin hopped atop the young man's pinto and galloped across the field.

Running Deer swiftly approached Joe Vann's large two-story brick mansion decorated with natural colored carvings of blue, red, green and yellow. The home had been built by Joseph's father, James, in 1804. Joseph inherited it along with his father's various businesses in

1809, when his father was shot for having killed one too many men in his drunken frenzies.

Outside the house were several covered wagons and teams of horses. Dozens of slaves carried items from the house and placed them inside the wagons while Joseph's wives, Polly, Unk, and Jennie, mournfully gathered their children about their skirts.

Running Deer fastened his horse in front of the house and climbed the steps two at a time, dodging two men carrying a rocking chair out to the wagon. Inside the drawing room, Running Deer found the Chief directing men in their task of vacating the house.

"Chief!" Running Deer called breathlessly. "What has happened? Why are you leaving?"

"It seems I've broken a horrible law, Running Deer," Joseph Vann answered sarcastically.

"What law? You are a good honorable man. You've broken no law," Running Deer defended.

"It seems the state of Georgia has passed a law without my knowledge that states that a Cherokee cannot hire a white man. I, as you know, hired a white overseer just this past week."

"And they'll confiscate your land for this?"

Joe nodded, angrily pursing his lips, "Either I leave or they'll attack my family and the village."

"It's not right. It's thievery plain and simple! Thievery, I say!" Running Deer exclaimed, sliding his fingers angrily through his thick black hair.

"I know," Joseph patted his young friend's shoulder comfortingly. "We'll take our things and start again. Worry not. We shall be well. Take care of yourself and your family, and mind your back."

"Yes, Sir," Running Deer nodded, observing the Chief's kind eyes as he forced a sad smile.

"Where will you go?"

"For now, we'll cross the border into Tennessee. We have another home there."

Running Deer's eyes surveyed the emptying household, "How can I help?" Joe Vann thanked Running Deer and set him to work carrying items from the house.

Jillian led the horse packed with supplies through the village. Her heart heavy and tears threatening, she visited the widows and the poor, bringing them much needed blankets and supplies for the storm that brewed on the horizon. Everywhere she went the villagers spoke of Joe Vann and the evil white men who drove him from his lands. The snow descended in greater density as she stepped out of the home of an elderly widow.

As she started back down the road, her seventeen-year-old sister Elizabeth ran toward her. Elizabeth's black hair billowed in the wind, and she tugged a pelt around her shoulders, nose and mouth. Her rosy red cheeks jutted above the fur, and she squinted to keep the snow from settling in her deep brown eyes.

"Jillian! There's a man with a wagon at the village entrance who says he has supplies for you."

"Oh, Mr. Whitmore," Jillian nodded. She had dispersed all the provisions from the back of the horse, so she motioned for Elizabeth to join her, and they both climbed atop the animal. Jillian nudged the paint's ribs and trotted in the direction of the village entrance.

"He is every bit as handsome as you described, Jillian," Elizabeth smiled as she clung to her sister's waist for support.

Jillian giggled, "He is, is he not? I fear I am as transparent as glass in his presence. Pray I learn to control my emotions where that merchant is concerned."

"I shall pray his heart is as transparent to you as yours is to him," Elizabeth replied. "Then you shall know how to proceed."

"You are wise beyond your years, my dear sister."

"What wisdom I have, I have gleaned from observing you, dear Jillian," Elizabeth patted her sister's arm lovingly.

"I fear wisdom flees me in that man's presence."

"Then I shall pray that your wisdom returns."

"From your lips to God's ears, sweet sister."

When Jillian and Elizabeth arrived, they found Jesse in the front of his wagon with two little boys and a little girl sitting on either side of him. They were busily chattering away to him in Cherokee, and he did his best to speak to them. He knew a little of the language, but not enough to fully understand their words. His kind eyes smiled at them, and he pulled a handful of licorice whips from inside his vest and handed them each a piece of candy. They squealed with delight and munched eagerly on the black lace.

"A glimpse inside his soul perhaps?" Elizabeth whispered into her sister's ear. A smile graced Jillian's lips as she nodded slightly in agreement.

Jesse's eyes lifted from the children to find Jillian and Elizabeth sitting atop the horse. He smiled and nodded. Jillian returned the greeting, and then her eyes went to the vehicle he drove. She'd never seen anything like it. She'd seen canvas-covered wagons, but Jesse's wagon looked like a large wooden box mounted to a traditional buckboard. He and the children sat under a wooden shelter that opened toward the team of four horses.

"Run along little ones," Jillian kindly ordered the children in their native tongue, and watched them hop down from the wagon and scurry off toward their homes. Her attention then turned to the merchant.

"I realize I promised you a stroll, Mr. Whitmore, but," her eyes turned skyward, "with this storm coming, it is imperative that I distribute these provisions to the sick and the elderly. Perhaps we may take that stroll another day."

"I understand," he nodded. "I will help you make your deliveries instead."

"I do not wish to trouble you, Sir. We can unload the supplies here and then deliver them in trips with the horse."

"Nonsense. You'll catch your death of cold, and we can get the provisions to those who need it faster if I drive."

Jillian turned toward her sister who still sat behind her, "Elizabeth, please take Running Deer's horse back to our place, and I'll ride with Mr. Whitmore to make the deliveries." Elizabeth agreed with a knowing smile, and Jillian hopped down.

Jesse descended from the wagon and helped Jillian into the front seat. He climbed in beside her, asked her where she wanted to go first and then cracked the reins.

Their first stop was to visit an elderly widow. Jesse marveled at the well tended home. All of the homes they passed appeared to be in good repair.

"This is a very attractive village," Jesse noted with surprise in his voice.

"We are not savages, Mr. Whitmore," Jillian's eyebrows furrowed with disappointment.

"I - I did not mean to imply that you were, Miss Elliott." Jesse's expression grew serious. "I just meant that this is a very nice village - I haven't seen many like it - white or otherwise, kept in such good order as this one."

"We believe in taking care of what God has given us."

"God? Not the Great Spirit?"

Again she heard the surprise in his voice. "Many of us in the village- especially those of us in the rising generation - are Christians, Mr. Whitmore."

"I didn't realize."

"Chief Vann's father encouraged the Moravian missionaries to teach our people. Many accepted Christian ways, but that is not necessarily why we take care of what God has given us. It has been the Cherokee way long before the missionaries arrived. We take care of what we have, and we take care of one another."

"Admirable," he helped her descend from the wagon and went to the back to open the hinged door.

"I have never seen a wagon like this before," she placed her hand on the side of the wooden structure.

"I built it myself. With as much as it rains around here and as many deliveries as I have to make, I needed something sturdy that could withstand the elements and protect the merchandise."

He held the door open for her, and she ascended the steps on the back that led up into the wagon. She noted that the left side of the vehicle was filled with firewood while the right held her provisions. She selected the food and blankets she would need for the widow and handed some of them to Jesse and carried the rest herself.

Two brown eyes with leathery laugh lines stretching out to either side peered mummy-like from the mound of pelts wrapped around the woman's shoulders and head. She motioned them to step inside.

"It's too cold in here," Jillian noted pointing to the waning fire in the hearth. The elderly woman explained in her native tongue that she had run out of firewood and had neglected to ask anyone to help her chop more. Jillian sat the woman down in a chair and piled blankets over her body to keep her warm. Just as she was telling the woman that she would find a young man to come bring her some firewood, Jesse entered the house carrying an armload of logs. He went straight to the fireplace that contained only the low embers of a previous fire and rekindled the flame, adding more logs until a large fire glowed.

The elderly woman thanked him in her native tongue and he responded in what little Cherokee he knew, telling her that she was most welcome. Jillian set to work fixing a meal while Jesse sat next to the woman listening to her rattle on in a language he could barely understand. He simply nodded and smiled when she smiled and his handsome face took on concern as the woman's conversation grew more serious.

The woman embraced them both as they left and once they'd climbed back into the wagon, Jillian turned to Jesse, "You understood not a word she spoke, did you?"

"Well, perhaps one or two," he chuckled.

Jillian giggled and pulled her pelt securely around her shoulders and over her mouth and nose.

"What was the story she told that made her so sad and angry?"

"It was about Chief Vann," she replied.

"What has happened to him?"

"He and his family are being driven from their home. They must be gone by morning."

"Why? What happened?" Jesse asked anxiously.

"The only thing I heard was that the State says he's broken a law, and they are confiscating his property. He and his family must evacuate by morning."

"It sickens me sometimes to be a white man," Jesse mumbled more to himself than to her.

She put her hand comfortingly on his hand that rested on his knee. "We know all white men aren't dishonest thieves, Mr. Whitmore."

Jesse looked down at her hand and placed his other hand atop her slender bronze fingers and squeezed gently. "Thank you, Miss Elliott. I appreciate that."

Realizing the forwardness of her action, she retrieved her hand and placed it beneath her fur coat. "We better go. We have several more deliveries."

The next place they visited was a small home of an expecting mother.

"This is my friend Martha," Jillian pointed to the young woman who appeared to be Jillian's age. "Her husband is away hunting for furs." She then introduced Jesse to her friend in Cherokee. The young woman smiled delightedly and opened the door wider for them to enter.

Jesse set the supplies on the table, and Jillian embraced her friend and placed her hand on her rounded belly. "Martha's baby is due in midsummer," Jillian told Jesse. "It's her first."

Jesse smiled and offered his congratulations.

"We grew up together," she added.

Martha spoke to Jillian in Cherokee, and the two young women giggled like schoolgirls. Somehow Jesse had the feeling he could be the object of their conversation, but he didn't understand anything they said well enough to be certain.

Jillian embraced her friend once again and started for the door. Martha bid Jesse farewell, and the pair returned to the wagon to deliver more supplies. Each place they stopped, everyone seemed to know and love Jillian. For many she was their angel of mercy, bringing them their very means of survival. In each home with a dying fire or a low supply of fuel, Jesse unloaded an armful of firewood, stoked their fires, and left more for the days to follow.

By the time they had completed their rounds it had grown dusk, and Jillian noticed that Jesse had liquidated his entire supply of firewood. She turned toward him as they sat in the front of the wagon. "I fear it may be a week or two before we can reimburse you for the firewood, Mr. Whitmore."

"You owe me nothing for the firewood," he shook his head negatively.

"But, it is only right that we should pay. I hope we did not take wood you planned to deliver to another!" she suddenly realized that he probably intended to deliver it to a customer after dropping off her supplies.

"No, I bartered some cornmeal, oil, and flour with a lumberman on the way here. I was just going to use it at the store."

"Still, you needed it. We must pay."

"No, you didn't ask for it. I gave it. Besides, this worked out just as well, because I needed the wagon emptied before I go see Joe Vann."

"You're going to see the Chief?"

"Yes, I'll take you home and then head over there. Which way to your house?"

She pointed him in the right direction and added, "Why are you going to see Joe Vann?"

"With this snow coming down like this, I reckon he could use a sheltered wagon for his family. He's been a kind friend to me, and it's time to return the favor."

If his kind and gentle nature in caring for the old and the sick had not already impressed her, his devotion to his friend would.

Jesse took Jillian home and helped her down from the wagon.

"Now remember," he said, pointing his finger toward her, a serious expression on his handsome face, "You still owe me a stroll."

"Perhaps on a prettier day," she smiled.

"Just be aware that I plan to collect on our barter sooner rather than later."

"Yes sir," she waved as he climbed back up into his wagon and rode toward Joe Vann's.

Joe Vann drove his wagon while Jesse cracked the reins on his own. The Chief's family huddled securely within the back of the merchant's wagon with their furniture, the wives and children wrapped securely in mounds of quilts, pelts and blankets. A single lantern hung from a hook on the interior wall, offering a dim light for the family as they traveled through the snowy bitter cold toward the Tennessee border, never to return to their beautiful home again.

Chapter Four

Jillian opened the front door to find Running Deer standing outside. "I can't believe he's gone," Running Deer mumbled. Jillian motioned him into the house and put her arms comfortingly around her cousin. Ever since Running Deer's father had died, Joe Vann had taken him under his wing and treated him as if he were one of his own.

"I hate them all," he bellowed angrily. "Every last one of them's a gold digging thief!"

"I realize you're angry, Running Deer, but we must not judge an entire race by a few rotten apples."

"A few?" he quipped sarcastically. "They're all thieves, encroaching on our lands. We've been here for thousands of years, and then they come along, set up their government to overthrow ours - passing illogical secret laws and then throwing us off our lands should we innocently break them!"

Jillian looked somberly out the window. She knew Running Deer had a right to be angry, but hate would only eat a man up inside. It didn't hurt your enemy to hate him, it only hurt you. Besides, all white men weren't evil. She could think of at least one who was quite the opposite.

"You're thinking of that merchant, aren't you?" Running Deer observed.

Jillian's head darted toward him, surprised at how closely her cousin could read her thoughts. Of late, she wondered why the villagers had entrusted their negotiations to her. She seemed to be completely lacking in all ability to conceal her innermost thoughts! Especially where a certain merchant was concerned!

"You realize he's only after the treasure, do you not, Jillian? You come into that store with Joe Vann, always carrying silver in your purse. He thinks you know the location of Joe Vann's treasure and that if he woos you, you'll lead him straight to it!"

"You are mistaken, Running Deer."

"Mistaken? I think not. They're all money grubbing thieves, and the sooner you realize that, the better off you'll be. You're a smart woman, Jillian, but if you lose your head over this man, you're liable to end up getting yourself hurt and betraying our people in the process!"

"I would never do such a thing, Running Deer, and you know it well!" she spat angrily.

After several silent minutes had passed, Running Deer's voice softened. "I am sorry, Jillian. I didn't mean to imply that you couldn't be trusted. Besides, you don't even know where the treasure is," he patted her shoulder. "I'm sorry for my anger. It's not your fault. It all just makes me feel so helpless."

"I know, cousin, I know," she turned and put her arms around him, offering him what little consolation she could.

~*~

It would be an unseasonably warm mid-January afternoon before Jesse Whitmore came to collect on his debt. He rode into the village on a shiny black horse and ventured straight to Jillian's home. He wrapped the reins around a post, removed his hat and rapped cheerily on the front door.

Elizabeth answered, her eyes lighting with recognition, "Jillian isn't here right now. She's gone to visit the widows with mother. They left only a short time ago."

"Do you know which direction she traveled?"

"She went that way," Elizabeth pointed to her right.

"Thank you, Miss," he nodded and replaced his hat. He mounted his horse and galloped down the road in the direction Elizabeth had indicated.

After traveling a short distance, he observed Jillian emerging from a little home on his left. He reined in his horse, and Jillian looked up to see Jesse wearing a gray wool suit, a handsome hat and a neatly trimmed beard. He pulled his hat from his brow and rested it in his hands in front of him on the saddle.

"Good afternoon, Miss Elliott," he smiled.

"Good afternoon, Mr. Whitmore," she returned the greeting and approached his horse. Her mother stepped out of the house and noticed her daughter conversing with the handsome stranger. She joined her daughter, and looked toward Jesse astride his horse.

"Good day, Ma'am," Jesse addressed Mrs. Elliott.

"Mother, this is Mr. Whitmore from the trading post. Mr. Whitmore, this is my mother, Sophia Elliott."

Jesse smiled at Sophia. He could see where Jillian obtained her beautiful softened features. Jillian, only being a quarter Cherokee, possessed many of the European qualities of her grandparents.

"We were just visiting the widows," Jillian explained.

"May we help you with anything, Mr. Whitmore?" Sophia asked.

"Actually, it was such a pretty day, I took the afternoon off from work to collect on a debt," his eyes were smiling at Jillian, but the corners of his mouth did not rise.

Sophia noted the sparks between her daughter and the young merchant, "Do we owe Mr. Whitmore a debt?"

"I do," Jillian answered plainly.

"Then, you best pay it. You know how your father feels about honoring our obligations."

"Yes, Ma'am, I'll take care of it," Jillian could feel the flushed heat rising to her cheeks.

"I can wait if you have things to do," Jesse offered.

"Mother, would you mind continuing on without me while I tend to this matter of business?"

"I'll not mind in the least, my dear. You run right along."

"Now will be fine, Mr. Whitmore," Jillian told him in a businesslike tone.

"Very well," Jesse reached out his hand, and Jillian climbed onto the back of his horse. He nudged the equine's ribs, and it bolted so suddenly that Jillian reflexively clutched his waist. The horse galloped down the road a few feet, and then Jesse suddenly redirected the animal into an open field. They rode swiftly across the meadow, over a hill and toward the river.

Jillian pressed her cheek to his back and inhaled the sweet scents of peppermint, witch hazel, and a wood-burning stove. She realized she'd grabbed hold of him so suddenly that her hand had slipped inside his coat and clung to his shirt beneath. She could feel the muscles in his chest ripple as he pulled the reins to bring the horse to a halt.

He hopped down and put his hands to Jillian's waist, helping her descend. She knew well how to ride and to ascend or descend a horse, but she loved the way he so gallantly assisted her in such matters. Of course, any chance to come into direct contact with him made her heart swell with an exhilarating thrill.

"This looks like a lovely place for a stroll," he extended his arm to her, and she took it.

They walked along the bank of the river for several silent moments. "Thank you again for helping me with my deliveries and for the firewood."

"You're most welcome," he glanced at her with a smile and continued walking.

"Were you able to reach the Chief before he left?"

"Yes, I drove him and his family into Tennessee and saw them settled in a second home the Chief owns in Ooltewah. The Chief is a wise and resourceful man. They'll not keep him down long. In a few months, he plans to transport his family West aboard his steamboat."

"I hope we may all be as resourceful and wise." There was a sad and doubtful tone to her voice that Jesse did not miss.

He stopped and turned toward her. "Is there something wrong?"

"Threats, warnings," Jillian shook her head. "Without Joe Vann, the people are afraid, and those who want our lands seem to sense it like a coyote stalking for the kill."

"What kind of threats?"

"Three men rode into the village with papers claiming they'd acquired our lands through the state land lottery. The men of our village sent them away."

"Oh, I've heard about the land lottery," Jesse shook his head in dismay.

"I don't see how the state can lottery off lands that our people have lived on for centuries! What right do they have?"

"They have no right. Stealing is all it is. Perhaps you and your family should resettle? I would be happy to help you find a safer location away from the gold and silver mines that are rumored to be along this river. That's what they want, you know. They want to drive your people away so they can steal your precious metal mines."

"I know," she nodded. "It's all happening the way Chief Vann knew it would."

"Then leave." He put his hands on her shoulders. "Let me speak with your father and mother, and we'll find a safer place for you."

"Will you find a safer place for our entire village? We're a tribe, you know, we're all family."

Jesse grew more pensive, and then determination infused his face, "If I have to, yes, I'll find a place big enough for you all."

Jillian's eyes twinkled, and the corners of her lips rose at his willingness to help. She put her hand to his chest and patted it twice, "It's kind of you to want to help, but this is our home. The council will not abide by worthless pieces of paper issued by state land lotteries. It will be all right in the end."

"I hope you're right," he put his hand over hers and held it to his chest. In his heart, he knew she fooled herself. It was only a matter of time before the Cherokee were driven from their lands, and he determined at that moment that he would take it upon himself to see that Jillian and her family would not become casualties along the way.

His gaze was too penetrating, too intimate, and she retrieved her hand from his and started walking again. He followed her, extended his arm, and she laced her arm through his and changed the subject, "How is business?"

"It's doing very well," he smiled. "It's doing so well, that I believe I'll have enough saved by fall to build a fine home and think about settling down and raising a family."

Jillian's chest tightened at his remark. With whom would he be settling down and raising a family?

"I'm happy for you," was all she could think to say.

A grin turned up the corners of his mouth as he glanced at her, "Thank you." He stopped and turned toward her. "Would you be happy for yourself?"

"Pardon me?"

"Would you be happy to be the one settling down in the fall to raise a family?"

Jillian could feel her pulse throbbing in her long and slender neck. Her mouth went utterly dry, and she tried to swallow, but it was most difficult - especially with him looking at her that way. What was he asking? He waited patiently for her reply, but she had no idea how to answer the question.

Finally she spoke. "I would be happy to raise a family someday, if that is what you inquire, Mr. Whitmore."

Jesse chuckled, looked down at his boots and back toward her striking brown eyes. "Would you have anyone in particular with whom you'd like to raise a family?"

Jillian swallowed hard as her heart hammered within her bosom. How was she supposed to answer this question? She wasn't even sure of his feelings for her. Dare she share hers for him and take the chance of humiliating herself? What if he had someone else in mind for himself and was simply making conversation?

"I am not betrothed to anyone, if that is what you ask," she shook her head negatively.

"That is good to know," a delightful twinkle glimmered in his green eyes.

"Are you?" she countered.

"Am I what?"

"Betrothed?"

"No," he chuckled, "Not at the moment."

She turned from him and began walking back in the direction they had come so that he could not see the glowing smile spread across her face.

He took a few quick steps to catch up with her and asked, "Where are we going?"

"Would you care to join our family for supper this evening, Mr. Whitmore?" she asked without turning toward him, only continuing to walk.

"I -" he looked toward her quizzically. "I suppose I could. Thank you. Yes."

"Good, because it's time I returned to help with supper."

Sophia and John Elliott sat down to the dinner table with their younger children and Mr. Whitmore while Jillian and Elizabeth set the food on the table.

"We're glad you joined us this evening, Mr. Whitmore," Sophia smiled at the merchant.

"Yes, I've known your uncle Welt for quite some time and am pleased to get to know his nephew," John Elliott added. "Your uncle drives a hard bargain."

"I'm afraid you'll be a bit disappointed if you expect me to be cut from the same cloth as Uncle Welt," Jesse frowned.

"I was surprised to see your uncle sell the mercantile," John reached for a bowl of stewed potatoes.

"He helps out now and then so I can take days off - like today - and I appreciate that," Jesse's expression was so somber that Jillian had an odd feeling cross over her.

"What does he do with the rest of his free time?" Mr. Elliott asked.

"He's taken to fortune hunting," Jesse rolled his eyes.

"Fortune hunting?" John's gaze darted toward his daughter whose face suddenly grew pale and frightened.

That's what this was all about! she decided in that heart-pounding, horrible moment. He was always dropping comments about the gold and silver mines, acting friendly toward Joe Vann and prying into her life without really showing a marked interest in her. Running Deer was right! He was a gold digger - setting his sights on her only so she'd lead him to the treasure!

"Crazy – huh?" Jesse smirked, and then his eyes caught Jillian's as she returned an icy cold stare.

Mumbling an excuse, she rose from the table and crossed to the kitchen and leaned her hands on the counter. Her chest constricted, and it felt as if her breathing passageway had completely closed. How dare he sit there talking so casually about his fortune-hunting uncle! He was the fortune hunter! She cringed at the thought of how close they'd been to Joe Vann's treasure that day by the falls. Had he taken her there because he suspected she'd know exactly where to find the treasure? Did he think something in her expression or words would betray the secret? Or did he assume she'd simply blurt out the location and betray her people outright?

When Jillian did not return to the table for several minutes, her mother rose from her seat and went to the kitchen, putting her hands on her daughter's shoulders.

"Are you well, dear?"

"I'm feeling quite ill, Mother. Would you please bid my farewell to Mr. Whitmore? I need to lie down." Jillian did not wait for a reply but hurried up the steps to her bedroom, down the hall and shut the door behind her.

"I'm sorry, Mr. Whitmore. Jillian has fallen suddenly ill and has gone to lie down. She asked me to extend her farewell."

Jesse rose from his chair and stared toward the steps he'd seen Jillian so abruptly ascend. "I'm sorry. Is there anything I can do to help?"

"No, please sit down, Mr. Whitmore, and finish your meal."

Reluctantly Jesse returned to his chair and tried to carry on a polite conversation when his mind was on Jillian and that terse look she'd shot him. If looks could maim, that one would have removed a few appendages! What had he said?

Jillian lay curled on her bed, tears flooding her eyes. How stupid could she have been? She never should have peeked from beneath the blindfold! Now she knew for certain the location of the treasury. What if he'd read it in her eyes that day at the falls? No, she hadn't known the location for certain then, thank heavens!

She should have paid attention to Running Deer's warning. He was right all along! She should have known Whitmore's politeness and willingness to give away all that firewood was for a purpose. No merchant as shrewd as everyone purported Mr. Whitmore to be would have so freely given away such valuable merchandise! He did want something in return – he wanted her to tell him where the treasure was!

A loud thundering rumble rattled the frame of the house and rain descended in torrents, bouncing noisily on the roof. She lay there for several hours, berating herself - angry one moment and shedding mournful tears the next. She felt like such a fool!

Slowly her bedroom door opened, and Elizabeth crept into her room, slipped off her dress, put on her nightgown, and climbed in bed next to Jillian.

"Why are you sleeping in here?" Jillian asked groggily.

"Mr. Whitmore is sleeping in my room," Elizabeth pulled the covers up around her neck.

"What? Why is he sleeping in your room?" Jillian sat up in the bed.

"It's a horrible thunderstorm, Jillian. Didn't you hear it? Father suggested he stay the night."

Jillian hated the blend of emotions that suddenly surged through her body. First there was a wonderful thrill that he would be sleeping under the same roof. Immediately she rebuked herself for even thinking such a thing. He was a lying thief - just like Running Deer said! Could she even trust him to stay in her home overnight? Then again, what could he do? There certainly was no treasure hidden inside their home. They were safe enough, but she didn't like the idea of Whitmore getting chummy with her family - so chummy they'd invite him to stay overnight.

She stood up, draped a quilt around her shoulders and started for the door.

"Where are you going?" Elizabeth asked.

"The outhouse," Jillian replied.

She hated to venture outside in the pouring rain, but she didn't have much choice. Quietly, she crept down the steps, toward the back door and quickly ran across the back yard to the outhouse. Afterwards, she scurried home, opened the door and ran squarely into the solid chest of a man standing in the darkness just inside the door.

"Oh," she squealed.

"I'm sorry, I didn't mean to startle you," he whispered as his powerful arms encircled her waist.

Recognizing his voice instantly, she pushed herself from him.

"You scared me half to death!"

"I'm sorry. Are you feeling better?"

"I'm fine," she snipped.

He put his hands gently on her shoulders, "Have I done something wrong?"

"Let me go," she pushed at his hands, attempting to remove them.

"What's going on, Jillian?" He let his hands drop to his side. "One minute you're asking me to dinner and the next you're as cold as the Tennessee River on a winter's morn."

"Do not speak so familiarly with me, Mr. Whitmore," she barked.

"Whatever I did or said, it's truly sorry I am for it," he sounded so sincere. But she could not - would not waver. She must stand firm. She knew what he was up to now.

"You're not sorry. You're just sore that I'm not going to fall into your snare."

"What snare? You're not makin' a lick of sense."

"You're nothin' but a lying treasure-hunting thief!"

"What?"

"You're just trying to befriend me so I'll tell you where Joe Vann's treasure is! I can see right through you, Mr. Whitmore, and I'm not going to fall for it! Running Deer warned me about you, and I was too blind to listen to him!"

"Listen to me, Jillian," he grabbed her shoulders once more. "I care not the least for Joe Vann's treasure! I do, on the other hand, care a great deal for you." His hand went to her cheek caressing it gently.

She grabbed his wrist and tugged his hand from her face. The clouds drifted away from the moon, and now she was no longer barking at darkness, instead his magnificent presence boldly stood before her. She almost wavered, almost weakened, as the angry pounding of her heart was replaced with a thrilling flutter. Steeling her emotions she continued, "Don't lie to me, Mr. Whitmore. You admitted at dinner that you and your uncle were treasure hunters. You're always asking me about the gold and silver mines, befriending Joe Vann, sniffing around here trying to learn about my private life so you can bait me into telling you where the treasure is. I've news for you, Mr. Whitmore; I have no idea where that treasure is so there's not a thing to woo out of me!"

She wasn't making a bit of sense as far as Jesse could tell, but the way the moonlight danced in her angry eyes and the raindrops glistened on her silky brown skin made her simply irresistible. The only thing he wanted to do was to gather her up into his arms and kiss her. So that's exactly what he did. He pulled her to him, leaned over and kissed her so boldly and overwhelmingly that her initial protests to push him away soon subsided, and her entire body went limp as a wet dishrag in his powerful arms.

"You're wrong you know," Jesse mumbled into her ear as he held her against him. Jillian simply nodded affirmatively and her hands, which rested on his bearded cheeks, pulled his mouth towards hers once more. Jesse's strong arms encompassed her, and he pulled her tighter to him. He was astonished at how the rage that had poured from her lips only a few moments prior had so quickly transformed into emblazoned fervor.

He put his palms to her cheeks and looked squarely into her eyes, "You realize that I would never ask you to betray your people."

"I know, I'm sorry," she whispered breathlessly, and her warm mouth melted into his once more as her heart hammered within her bosom. She was losing control. He could sense it, and if he didn't stop what was happening between them, he feared what they might give into on this dark, cold, rainy night. He stepped back from her, holding her at arm's length. He leaned over to pick up her quilt, which had fallen to the floor, and draped it around her shoulders. She self-consciously pulled it around herself.

Suddenly, she turned her back to him. "I'm sorry," she mumbled, horrified at her own behavior. "I know not what possessed me." She put her hands to her cheeks to cool the heat that surged through her body and sent tingles throughout her extremities.

"It's all right, I understand."

"You do?"

"It was a long time in coming," he whispered.

"I am sorry," she replied softly.

"Be not remorseful. I rather enjoyed it," he chuckled.

"I meant about accusing you of being a gold-digging thief."

"Oh, that? Even my uncle charged me with no less."

"He did?" she turned back around to see the expression in his eyes.

"He said I was using you to find the treasure. But he's the one who wants the treasure, Jillian. I want no part of it. All I want is - is you."

"Me?"

"You," he stared lovingly into her eyes. "That's what I tried to ask of you today while we were walking, but I muddied it. I was trying to learn if you've been promised to another - perhaps a Cherokee brave. When you said you hadn't, I almost asked you right then, but I wavered. After all, I haven't even asked your father."

"Almost asked me what?" her heart pounded so wildly she could hear it drumming in her ears.

"What would you think of marrying someone like me?"

Was it true? Had he truly asked her to marry him? To be his? Would the man who sent her emotions flying in all directions be hers for the taking? Jillian stepped toward him and put her hands to his cheeks. His beard was soft. She'd expected it to be scratchy, but it wasn't. It felt wonderfully warm and cozy. She felt tears brimming in her eyes, and she choked back the lump that had formed in her throat, "I - I'd be honored to be your wife."

"Good, because you're all I think about, Jillian Elliott, and I want you for my bride," he whispered just before his lips met hers once more, leaving her weak kneed and breathless.

The next morning, Jillian rose earlier to prepare breakfast for her family and their guest. Her father awakened next to milk the cows and feed the animals. He entered the kitchen and put his hand to Jillian's shoulder.

"Are you feeling better, my daughter?"

"Thank you, Father, I am feeling much better."

"Good," he smiled and reached for a piece of bread and walked out the door to tend to his chores.

Jillian continued to prepare the meal until she heard footsteps descending the stairs. She turned toward the sound, and a smile spread across her cheeks, then she looked away shyly and back toward Jesse. The memory of the prior evening's encounter came flooding back and suddenly she felt unusually timid.

"Good morning," he greeted her.

"Good morning."

He stepped toward her and pointed to the meat she'd fried and set aside, "May I?"

"Help yourself," she gestured.

"Has your father risen?" he inquired.

"Yes," she answered nervously. He was going to ask him now! Her insides set to trembling. "He's outside with the animals."

"Then, wish me luck," he winked, popped a bite of meat in his mouth and headed for the door.

John Elliott sat on a stool milking his wife's favorite cow. He heard Jesse approach and greeted him jovially. Jesse returned the morning ritual and leaned on the doorway of the barn.

"Sir, I'd like to ask you something if I may?"

"Yes," John nodded and continued to express the milk from the cow.

"I'm very fond of your daughter, Jillian, Sir." He twiddled a piece of grass nervously in his fingers. "Actually, you could say, I'm quite smitten with her, and... I wondered... You see, by fall I should have saved enough money for a homestead, and..." He knew he stammered too much when he was nervous so he decided to just blurt it out, "Sir, I would like to ask for your daughter's hand in marriage."

John Elliott chuckled at the young man's uneasiness, and then his expression grew more serious, "You have my permission, Mr. Whitmore. Whether you obtain Jillian's shall depend upon whether you can tame that angry fire I saw kindled in her eyes last evening. I know not what you said or did to set her off, but Jillian only vacates a room in such a manner when she's trying to contain her rage."

A tight-lipped smile turned up the corners of Jesse's mouth. "You know your daughter very well, Sir."

"That I do," John nodded, with a slightly amused twinkle in his eye.

"I believe we've resolved the problem, Sir." Jesse tipped his hat, "Thank you for your permission, Sir."

"You're welcome," he smiled, turned his attention back to his task, and Jesse departed for the house with a spring in his step.

Chapter Five

A shrill, bloodcurdling scream rent the still morning air. Jillian bolted upright in her bed and ran to her door, down the steps and found her father at the threshold peering out. He looked left, then right. Suddenly three horses carrying dark-cloaked riders bolted from the right and sped past, flinging mud from their thundering hooves. John recognized the horses as those of the men who had brought deeds to the land issued by the state land lottery. He reached for his rifle mounted by the door and stepped outside. Immediately he darted in the direction the riders had come. He would have followed them, but he knew the owner of that scream, and he had to go to her.

His wife and children gathered at the door to see what had caused the commotion. The woman's scream turned to a cry of lamentation, a mournful death chant.

"I know that voice," Jillian's eyes lit with horrified recognition as they met her mother's.

"Jillian, don't go out there! Let your father see to it," Sophia cried, but Jillian did not heed the warning.

Immediately, she bolted out the door, her bare feet meeting the moist dew-saturated grass. Following her father, she arrived in front of the home of Running Deer and his mother, Waw-Li. The woman's body draped over her son, cradling his head tenderly in her lap and rocking back and forth.

As Waw-Li's eyes met Jillian's she cried, "He's gone! They've slain him! My son! Oh my sweet son!" Her tear-stained cheeks turned to John pleadingly.

Jillian beheld in horror the blood-soaked chest of her young cousin. He'd been beaten and stabbed and left dead at his mother's doorstep. Jillian fell to her knees, weeping, caressing the blood-matted locks.

John knelt to feel for a pulse. He turned to Jillian and shook his head negatively. Running Deer was gone! John put his arms consolingly around his brother's widow, and she leaned against his chest sobbing bitterly. "Who did this thing?" he inquired, not fully expecting an answer from the widow.

"I know not," the grieving mother cried, continuing to rock her son and lean against her brother-in-law.

Through her blurry tears, Jillian noted a parchment affixed to the side of the house with a blade.

"What is that?" she pointed.

John stood and ripped the parchment free. "It's in English. Please read it." He handed it to his daughter.

"It says that for every fortnight we remain, one of our youth shall die, and that if we wish to spare them, we must vacate our lands immediately."

"What?" John Elliot bellowed.

"Oh, John, where will we go? What shall we do?" Waw-Li wailed.

"That, I do not know," he offered numbly and reached down to lift his nephew and carry him into the house.

Three painful, gloomy, and fearful days passed. Even the heavens seemed to weep by casting torrential teardrops upon the land. The village buried Running Deer in the tribal burial grounds, and the family mourned. The council convened to make a decision. After much deliberation, some vying for staying and fighting, others wanting to search out the perpetrators, and still others voting to leave while they could, a decision was made.

Since Jillian was betrothed to a white man, the council decided that she should take tribal resources and travel with Jesse Whitmore to purchase new lands in McMinn County, Tennessee, where Sophia's family resided. In council they formulated a plan involving the merchant of which he was completely unaware. It would be Jillian's task to convince him to assist them, but she and her father felt certain he would comply. Some feared the man couldn't be trusted, but others who had seen him give his firewood voluntarily and assist the villagers on the night Joe Vann left, believed he was their best alternative. They had no choice. They needed a white man for the plan to work, and they must take a leap of faith and trust Jesse for the task.

~*~

Jillian lay in her bed listening to the crickets' song outside her window when light tapping sounded at her door.

"Who is it?" she inquired.

"It's me, Elizabeth," her sister replied.

"Come in."

Elizabeth, carrying a lamp, opened the door, closed it behind her and set the lamp on Jillian's bureau. "You looked like something was troubling you over dinner," she whispered as she sat on the foot of Jillian's bed.

"I'm just nervous about approaching Jesse tomorrow about the council's plan."

"He loves you. He'll do it; you needn't worry," Elizabeth assured.

"How do you know?" Jillian wished Elizabeth hadn't brought her lamp into the room so that her sister couldn't see the expressions of doubt and apprehension on her face.

"How do I know he loves you, or how do I know he'll participate in the plan?"

"Either."

"You can tell he loves you by the way he looks at you and treats you. As for the plan, any man who loves a woman as much as Mr. Whitmore loves you would gladly do anything within his power to save her and her family."

"You live in an idealistic world, Elizabeth. The white man's world isn't so simplistic. You never know what could occur. Just look at what happened to Running Deer," tears brimmed in Jillian's eyes at the mere mention of her friend.

"Mr. Whitmore isn't anything like those men who slew Running Deer, and you know it, Jillian! I'm surprised at you!"

"But how can I be absolutely certain? What if Running Deer is right, and Jesse is just pretending to love me for the treasure?" Jillian had never voiced her fear aloud, and the moment the words escaped her lips she felt the need to retract them, but it was already too late.

"Jillian Elliott! If you don't trust the man anymore than that, then why are you even marrying him? Why did you agree with the council's agenda if you doubted him so?"

"Because I love him," Jillian whispered.

"But surely you can't mistrust him so when your heart loves him?"

"I don't mistrust him. He's given me no reason to doubt him. But I just can't seem to put Running Deer's words from my mind. There's that gnawing, lingering remnant of uncertainty."

"What does your heart tell you? Does it say that you can trust Mr. Whitmore or not?"

Jillian sat in the silence that was broken only by the crickets' song. She sorted out her feelings and intuitions; trying to distinguish the fear Running Deer had planted in her mind against the reality of Jesse and their feelings for one another. Finally she spoke, "My heart tells me to trust him."

"Then trust him, Jillian. Your happiness depends upon it. Let the doubts and fears go. Let Running Deer go. What happened to him was horrible, but it has nothing to do with your relationship with Mr. Whitmore."

"You're right, you're absolutely right," Jillian sat up and patted Elizabeth's hand. "Thank you, Elizabeth."

"You're welcome. Try to put all these doubts out of your mind and get some sleep. You have a big day tomorrow." With that, Elizabeth stood, hugged her sister goodnight and left her room, taking her lamp with her.

~*~

The hot summer sun glistened off the crystal clear blue lake. Jillian blotted the perspiration from her brow with the back of her hand as she descended from her horse and tied it to a tree in a thicket. She'd sent word to the trading post for Jesse to meet her at the village entrance that evening. He wasn't even aware of her cousin's death or the threat to the village. She couldn't bring herself to write the words. She would tell him in person and seek his help face-to-face. But before she could do that, she needed to acquire the silver. Since Joe Vann and Running Deer were both gone, she'd have to retrieve it herself.

This was the first sunny day since Running Deer's murder and with the sun came hope, the first hope Jillian had felt since the horrifying loss. The ride and the bright weather renewed her energy and helped to restore her soul after enduring the most heartbreaking experience of her young life. A renewed sense of purpose surged through her. Her people needed her to be strong, to fulfill their plan, and she took comfort in knowing Jesse would be at her side every step of the way - at least she hoped he would. If he truly loved her he would do this with her, change their plans, alter his destiny for her and her people.

She stepped out of the brush, approached the shore and examined the waterfall. She'd traveled by land because she wasn't sure of the river route. The sweltering day called for a cool swim anyway. She unfastened her dress and let it drop to her ankles. In her undergarments she slipped into the water. It was cooler than she suspected so rather than ease in, she gracefully dived forward into the water and swam across the lake toward the falls.

The torrent of water plummeted from the steep cliff, bubbling into the froth below. When she reached the falls, rather than go through the violent flow, she waded to the side and pulled herself up onto a rock. Carefully, she stepped behind the waterfall and back into the cave.

She'd neglected to bring a torch and the cave was dark and dank. A little sunlight streamed through from the sides of the waterfall, illuminating a tinderbox at the mouth of the cave. She lifted the lid and found a set of flints. She lit a torch that had been tossed aside and carefully ventured back into the cavern. The moist mud squished between her toes, and the water flowed to her ankles. Finally she reached a dry rocky area and found the gold and silver treasure undisturbed. Perhaps there was less shimmering metal than she'd seen the first time she was here, but Joe Vann had probably removed what belonged to him.

The shiny gold coins caught Jillian's eye and a tempting urge swept over here to take just one of them, but remembering Joe Vann's warning, she resisted the impulse and moved toward a basket of silver. On second thought, for the amount of land they needed to purchase, she would need gold. It would take too much silver. She searched around, looking for loose nuggets instead of marked coinage. Finding what she needed, she pulled the leather pouch from her neck and filled it with the metal. She replaced the bulging pouch around her throat and ventured back to the mouth of the cave, extinguished the torch and tossed it to the earth.

For several moments she stood motionless behind the falls, observing the rushing liquid plunge into the foamy rapids. She inserted her hand and surprised that it did not sting from the force of its descent, she stepped forward, letting the powerful fluid sweep over her, massaging her neck, scalp and back. It felt divinely invigorating! She bathed there for some time, letting the cool soothing water rush over her body, rinsing away the pain, stress and fear.

Hot, tired and weary after a hard day's work, Jesse ventured to his favorite spot by the falls for a comforting swim. He sat down on a rock and liberated his toes from the constricting leather boots and woolen socks, pulled his shirt over his head and neatly folded his shirt and trousers and set them on a rock. He dove into the lake and swam to the center, leaning back, soaking his hair. Lifting his head from the water, he saw her standing in the falls. His breath caught. He knew she was beautiful, but never imagined she could be this striking! His heart raced as she swept her hair back, letting the water stream over her.

Jillian looked forward, and there in the lake was the object of her affection, clean-shaven and staring at her. Their eyes met for an instant, and she stepped back behind the falls. Panic swept over her. She must act normal! Quickly she slid the leather pouch around to her back and slipped it under her camisole. She had to appear as if she were only sunbathing. Her decision came quickly. She dove forward, through the falls and into the lake, swimming for some time beneath the surface, and ascending a few feet from Jesse.

"I suppose we had the same idea," she noted casually as she leaned back, and her hands wrung the water from her long shimmering locks. Now would not be the time to talk with him about Running Deer or the plan to save the village. She needed to escape him quickly so that he would not notice the gold-filled leather pouch and deduce the location of the treasure!

Self-consciously, Jesse looked down at his bare torso. Fortunately, he'd been in such a hurry to enter the cool water that he hadn't taken the time to remove his undergarments as he normally would.

"I – I didn't mean to disturb you. I - didn't know you were here," he stammered.

She'd never seen him so intimidated, and she released a slight giggle at his discomfort. Most women would have been appalled finding themselves in the water with a shirtless man, but Jillian had been around plenty of bare-chested braves. Unlike herself, she realized Jesse had most likely seen very few, if any, women in their undergarments.

"I've been here a while. I can leave so you can swim," she gestured toward the shore.

"Leave not on my account," he blurted, a little too hastily, he thought. He closed his eyes, and dipped his head under the water to cool his emotions. He emerged, swept the water from his face and tried to appear calm and collected. He felt like a schoolboy with his first crush, and he knew that the crimson he felt rising to his cheeks, betrayed the fact.

"Why, Mr. Whitmore, I believe this is the first time I've ever seen you flustered," she teased, and swam closer to him, dipping her mouth below the surface and letting the water spill from her lips.

He decided the girl was either a temptress or completely naïve. She stood directly in front of him now, and he felt as if his blood were simmering at a low rumbling boil. "Then again, maybe you better go if you know what's good for you."

"Oh, am I in danger, Mr. Whitmore?" she cut her eyes at him with a flirtatious grin, put a single index finger to his muscular chest and started to leave. "I'll see you at the village," she waved.

Jillian thought she'd climb ashore, dress and leave, but she got only a few feet before she felt Jesse's strong hand powerfully take possession of her waist. One palm caressed the center of her back, tugging her body flush with his while the other cradled her neck, his fingers lost in her thick ebony locks. His mesmerizing emerald eyes intimately possessed hers, sending her heart racing with the thrill of a thousand wild stallions set free in an open field. His gaze shifted in rapt worship of her every feature - her dazzling cinnamon eyes, her silky ebony tresses, strawberry lips, long slender neck, soft shoulders, and her bronze skin glistening with moisture. Finally, his adoration settled upon her mouth, and unable or unwilling to only observe, he took her lips in a powerful, driven kiss that left her perfectly and divinely overcome. Limp in his arms, her neck and shoulders became the beneficiaries of his controlled, yet emblazoned attention.

Abruptly, he released her and propelled himself back toward the center of the lake.

"Now go, and I better not find you here again until we're properly wed."

Speechless and dizzy, Jillian simply nodded breathlessly, her fingertips resting on the shoulder where his lips had been only a moment prior. Somewhat regaining her composure, she stepped ashore, dressed, and rode away.

Jillian paced nervously at the village entrance waiting for Jesse, a bit timid after their afternoon encounter, but more nervous about the plan she needed to explain to him. Would he be willing to set aside everything he had worked to build? Would he take the risks for her village? What if he agreed only out of obligation to her, and it drove a wedge between them? What if he called the entire engagement off because things had become too complicated? No, she wouldn't even think about the possibility. The man had stolen her heart; there was not a single remnant that he could not claim as his own. It was exhilarating to love and to be loved so completely, so thoroughly, but a part of her felt terribly vulnerable. Look what Jesse's people had done to Running Deer! She trusted Jesse. He wasn't like the others, yet an infinitesimal sliver of doubt surfaced in the most irritating moments - a thorn planted in her mind by Running Deer and driven deeper by his death. What if Jesse was only using her for the treasure?

No, she mustn't think that way. Her heart told her differently. She could see the love in his eyes. If Jesse didn't love her, he wouldn't have stopped what happened between them at the lake. A lesser man would have taken what he wanted and left her bereft of virtue.

Just as she forced away the traitorous thoughts, her eyes lifted to see the object of her contemplation riding toward her. A prayer formulated in her mind, pleading for help in obtaining the words needed to explain it all and win his aid. Merrily, he descended from his horse and embraced her.

"Thank you for coming," she smiled and took his hand.

Several people milled around the village within earshot of their conversation. "Here, let's walk." She pointed toward a field outside the village, and the pair ambled in that direction.

"It sounded urgent," his eyebrows furrowed quizzically.

"It is. I would have spoken with you about it at the lake, but..."

"It wouldn't have been a good time," he finished for her.

"No, you - we..."

"Were too distracted," his eyes fell nervously to his boots.

"Yes, we were too distracted," she agreed. She pointed to a fallen log and motioned for him to sit down. She remained standing and faced him as he sat. He motioned for her to join him, but she shook her head negatively. He was just too disturbing to sit next to as she tried to get through this. She paced in front of him for several moments, wringing her hands nervously with a somber expression on her face.

"Is everything all right, Jillian?" he asked, beginning to fear that she had become uncertain of her feelings for him. He shouldn't have pounced on her like that at the lake! He'd frightened her. Or, heaven forbid, maybe she found him unattractive? Yet, she didn't appear repulsed by him - quite the opposite. His mind began to wander as Jillian paced, working up her courage to begin.

"No, everything is not all right," she answered.

"I'm sorry about today, Jillian," he rose from the log and came toward her. "I was much too forward and got too..."

"No, Jesse, it's not what you're thinking," she smiled. "It's not about today," she motioned for him to sit back down.

"Are you sure? Because I promise I'll not do it again..."

She put her finger to his lips, "Shhh - Make no such promises, my love. Please, sit." She motioned for him to sit back down and reluctantly he backed toward the log.

"This isn't about today. It's about our village, about Running Deer." The mere mention of his name caused tears to pool painfully behind her eyelids.

"What's wrong?"

"Running Deer is dead, Jesse. Some white men on horses killed him and left him for dead in front of his mother's home."

"What?" He started to rise again to console her but she gestured for him to remain seated.

"Please, just let me get through this," she pleaded, brushing a tear from her cheek. "The killers left a threatening letter. It said that either our entire village evacuates or they will kill one of our youth every fortnight until we leave. We're certain it's the men who possess the land lottery deeds. They've taken matters into their own hands."

Jesse was having a very difficult time remaining seated. He wanted to run to her and hold her, but he forced himself to hear her out. "What will you do?"

"The council met and decided that we will take some of our treasure and purchase lands in McMinn County, Tennessee. My mother's father is not Cherokee. He and my grandmother have been urging Father and Mother to move near them and to purchase a five hundred acre tract of land that is for sale there. But my parents haven't had the funds for that on their own. Up until three days ago, Father was unable to persuade the council to leave. They fear that even if we move and purchase the land, the state will drive us from there as well."

Jesse's expression fell. "I am afraid they are right. Wherever the Cherokee own land, there will always be those who will find an excuse to steal it from them and drive them out."

"Yes, and so you see our dilemma. What we really need is to live on lands that are owned by someone who is not Cherokee - someone they would never attack - someone kind enough to let us stay there and make our home."

"And you have found someone who will do this for you?"

"We hope we have," she nodded.

"Make sure that whoever it is, he is a man who can be trusted and will not steal the land out from under you," Jesse warned.

"I believe he is such a man," she smiled at him in such a way that he felt uneasy. When she didn't continue, but her hope-filled eyes met his, Jesse swallowed the nervous lump in his throat.

"You're not talking about me are you?" he dubiously pointed his thumb to his chest.

"The council has agreed to make you an offer. We'll provide the gold. You purchase the land in your own name, and deed over portions to the villagers without actually recording the deeds with the state. As far as they're concerned you'll be the landowner. You can have a hundred acres for yourself for your trouble."

"Oh," his eyebrows rose. He thought for a moment and then sighed in relief. "It doesn't sound like I have much to lose with that arrangement." He shrugged and smiled at her.

"There's only one condition," she winced. He waited patiently for her to continue. "You have to live on the land."

"Why?"

"Because if you're not there, then if the state comes and finds Cherokee on your land, they'll drive them off, accusing them of squatting on another man's property. But if you're there, then you can protect them by saying that they are working your land for you."

Jesse put his hand to his chin pensively, "And this property is in McMinn County?"

"Yes"

"But I wouldn't be able to work my store all the way from McMinn County."

"I know. You'd have to sell the store, I suppose."

Jesse stood up and turned his back to her, took several steps and leaned his arm against a tree. She felt like her heart would pound out of her chest. Minutes passed like hours. Wringing her hands in the folds of her skirt, she wished he would say something - anything!

Finally, he slowly turned to face her. "I'll do it," he said somberly.

"Are you absolutely sure? I know it would mean giving up your dream that you've worked so hard for."

He stepped toward her and put one of his strong calloused hands on each of her shoulders, "I'll not be giving up my dream, Jillian. I'll be living it."

"But I thought it was your dream to own your store and..."

"And marry the girl I love and raise a family," he finished for her. "That's my dream, Jillian. The store is just a means to that end. With that much land we can farm, and I can sell the store and build a fine house for us. We can raise horses and cattle, and I can spend my time with you and our children instead of cooped up inside all day," he smiled excitedly.

"You mean this is what you want? You're not just agreeing because you feel pressured?"

"This is what I want," he nodded and kissed her lips briefly. She embraced him, thanking him for helping her people. Now there was only one more matter to discuss, and she hoped it went as easily as the last had.

"So, I suppose we're in a hurry to do this?" he asked as he stepped back slightly.

"Yes, the council wants me to go with you to buy the land immediately, and they will pack up the village, and we'll return for them when it's all arranged."

"Perhaps I can get my uncle to buy back the store. I think he misses it anyway. At least I should be able to get him to watch it for me while I'm gone," he mused. "So when do we leave?"

"In the morning."

"Just you and me?"

She nodded affirmatively, "We must carefully conceal that the land is being purchased for Cherokees."

"I understand."

"There's just one other small thing we need to discuss."

"What is that?"

"My parents insist that we marry before the trip."

Now Jesse felt a pounding in his throat that nearly set his head spinning! "You mean... before..." he stammered.

"Tonight" she nodded

"Tonight?" he gulped.

"My mother is insistent that propriety be observed. Also the council wishes us to be wed before the property is purchased." she explained with apologetic eyes.

"Because they do not trust me?" It was more a statement than a question.

"They don't know you the way I do. They would feel more comfortable if we were husband and wife when the land was purchased."

He tried not to show his apprehension, but it was all moving too fast! Of course he wanted to marry Jillian. He loved her and planned to marry her in the fall. But somehow reality set in at the thought of tonight. In the last five minutes he'd agreed to sell his store, move to a different state, and settle down with a village full of people with whom he couldn't even communicate! The freedom lover in him felt suddenly incredibly suffocated. He wanted to walk away as he had done before, to step back, think and regroup his thoughts, but he dared not hurt her feelings with such a move. She would interpret such an action as hesitance in marrying her, which really wasn't what the fear gripping every cell of his body was about right now.

Instead, he grabbed her and held her to him, letting her head rest on his chest as he looked past her into the trees and tried to collect himself. It would be all right. It really was his dream - just like he'd told her only a few minutes before. It was just happening so fast and furious and in ways he hadn't expected that it startled him. If he wanted to lay hold of it, he had to act now and push through the momentary fear.

"Let's do it," he said as he squeezed her a little tighter, and she breathed a sigh of relief.

"Is this really what you want, Jesse?" she leaned back to search his eyes.

He smiled, "Yes, this is really what I want. I'll admit it's happening a lot faster than I expected, but you're all I really want in life, and if I can have you tonight, then I am a lucky man indeed."

She took his cheeks in her palms, kissed him and then grabbed one of his hands and started walking, "We better get busy. My father already has the ham of venison because he knew you wouldn't have time to hunt one."

"Ham of venison?" he chuckled as she enthusiastically tugged him along, leading him back toward the village. He had to quicken his pace to keep up with her.

It's tradition. In the Cherokee ceremony the groom brings a ham of venison, and the bride offers an ear of corn. It's symbolic," she explained. "It's your job to provide for our household, and it's my responsibility to care for it and nourish those within it."

As they reached the village, Jesse helped her atop his horse and climbed in front. She excitedly explained the Cherokee wedding ceremony.

"We're really fortunate that a wedding was held only yesterday at the townhouse because the ground has already been blessed."

"Blessed?"

"Yes, the ground for the ceremony must be blessed for seven days before the wedding, but it's already been blessed."

"It sounds like I'll just have to follow your lead on all of this," he chuckled.

"It really is a beautiful ceremony," she smiled, and tightened her arms about his waist as the horse galloped onward to her home.

~*~

As the sun set in the west, Jillian and Jesse approached the sacred fire at the center of the townhouse, each of them covered with a blue blanket.

Jesse lovingly admired his beautiful bride, her long silky hair pulled back in the comb she'd purchased the day he first met her. Little did he know that day that in less than a year, he would be standing with her on sacred Cherokee ceremonial ground, encircled by her clan. Jesse tried unsuccessfully to understand the words as the elderly priest blessed each of the wedding participants and the guests. Jillian's mother and eldest brother John stood with her.

Songs were sung in Cherokee and the priest administered his blessing to the couple. The priest removed first Jesse's blue blanket and then Jillian's. Carefully, he draped the couple together under one white blanket, symbolizing the beginning of their new life together.

The priest said something that Jesse could not understand and then pointed to the ham he held in his hands. Jesse understood that it was time for him to give his bride the venison, and she gave him her ear of corn. After accepting each other's symbolic gifts, the priest held out a Cherokee Wedding Vase. The vessel held one drink but had two openings so that they could each sip from it simultaneously.

As Jesse looked across the vessel to his lovely wife, he couldn't keep from marveling at how blessed he was to find her. With her beside him, he knew that there was nothing that together they could not accomplish. Maybe he should tell her the truth about his real dreams and aspirations? He determined to consider it. Perhaps she would not find them as nonsensical as his family had.

Chapter Six

Just after sunset, the clan gathered around the newlywed couple to bid them a cheerful farewell. Jillian embraced her parents, brothers, and sisters. Martha, with her protruding belly, worked her way closer to the couple. "Be well, Jillian, and return to us soon."

"I shall. And you keep that babe snug inside you until I return," Jillian's eyes twinkled.

"Try, I shall," her friend smiled wearily as she rubbed her rounded stomach with one hand and the small of her back with the other.

John Elliott took Jesse's hand in a firm grip, "Take care of my girl."

"Yes, sir, I will," Jesse nodded. Jillian had already climbed atop her horse, so Jesse mounted his, tipped his hat toward his new family, and the couple started out on their adventure.

As they approached the trading post, Jillian asked her husband, "Do you think your uncle will mind watching the store for a while?"

"I hope not." But Jesse wasn't looking forward to the conversation. His uncle always managed to make him feel an inch high. He could be jovial and caring at times, but at others, he knew exactly what to say to twist the knife to cause the most gut-wrenching anguish.

They dismounted their horses and tied them in front of the mercantile. It was well after sundown when they arrived, but all the lamps were lit inside the establishment. Welt leaned his gray head on his fist, his elbow resting on the counter. His pale blue eyes wearily followed Chet LaSalle who meandered around the store fingering items, pulling them from the shelves and replacing them.

"Do ya want anything, Chet, or are you just tryin' my patience?" the old man finally huffed from his perch at the counter.

"I'm a lookin', I'm a lookin', I might be needin' somethin'," Chet waved his hand.

"If you'd be needin' somethin', you'd be knowin' it," Welt rolled his eyes and checked the clock on the wall. Welt's wearied stance drew erect when he saw Jesse enter the mercantile with his hand in Jillian's and her bag of belongings in the other. "I was wonderin' if you'd be comin' back tonight or stayin' in the village!"

Jesse turned a furrowed brow toward Chet who still ambled aimlessly through the mercantile. "Chet, I'm sorry, but it's well after closing. I must ask you to leave for now, but you're most welcome to come back and browse tomorrow."

The frumpy customer eyed Jillian from head to toe stepping toward her with a lascivious glint in his eyes. He licked his salivating chops, "If you'll be havin' merchandise the likes of this in your establishment, I most certainly will return tomorrow to ... browse."

Jesse stepped protectively in front of his wife, "My wife isn't for browsing, Chet."

"Wife?" Welt blurted and then clamped his mouth shut when Jesse's reprimanding stare burned a hole through his forehead.

"Now, if you will please be on your way, Chet," Jesse continued calmly.

"All right... all right... but I don't see how ye expect to make a livin' if ye drive all the customers away," the vagrant's hand slapped the air, and he exited the store. Jesse followed him, shut the door and bolted it.

"Wife?" Welt's voice was soft as he looked from Jesse to Jillian and back. "You got yourself hitched today, then?"

"Yes, Uncle, Jillian and I were married this evening in the village."

"Well, my, my, my...Welcome to the family," Welt extended his arthritic hand to his new niece, and she clasped it graciously.

"Jillian and I will settle in upstairs, and then I need to speak with you tonight about some business."

"I'll just wait down here fir ya. I have a bit of stockin' I can do."

Jesse nodded, took Jillian's hand and led her behind the counter toward the back of the mercantile and up a rickety set of narrow wooden stairs. The steps led to an equally constricted hallway. The wood creaked beneath their feet as they passed an open door on their left. Jillian peered in to see a quilt tussled bed, pillows thrown haphazardly, clothes draped over a chair and spilling lazily onto the hardwood floor. A muddy pair of work boots flopped over on the floor at the foot of the bed.

"My uncle's a mess," Jesse stated the obvious as they continued to the end of the hallway. His voice dropped to a whisper, "You should have seen what the store was like before I took it over."

"Oh, I remember," she nodded. "It was always so difficult to find what you needed."

Jesse opened his bedroom door. The comparison between his room and his uncle's was that of a calm spring morning to a catastrophic whirlwind. To say Jesse was tidy would have been an understatement. His full size brass bed was immaculately made, topped with a handsome burgundy and navy quilt. You could have eaten off his floor. There wasn't so much as a stray shoe under his bed. His dresser shined from polishing and only a simple burnished brass oil lamp sat on it. His washbasin sparkled. Jillian stepped inside, and Jesse set her bag in the center of his bed.

She noted his closet where his clothes were neatly arranged by type and color. His suits were hung together ordered from the darkest black to the lightest gray, his pants next in a similar manner. His white shirts were crisply starched and ironed and his shoes lay in an orderly fashion across the floor of the closet. She hated to inject her presence into the room and disrupt its tranquility.

"It's not much, but we'll only be here for the night. Make yourself at home while I go speak with my uncle."

Make myself at home? she chuckled. If she were at home, the bed wouldn't be made, and her closet would not be so sorted. Of course, her room didn't look like Welt's either - just some happy medium between the fastidious and the filthy. *How will I ever keep house to suit him?* she worried, nervously nibbling a fingernail. *Then again, maybe fortune will smile on me, and he'll do all the housekeeping!*

A bit lost, she looked around the room, trying to decide best what to do without disturbing her surroundings. Finally, she decided to find her nightgown and change for the evening. She opened her bag, rummaged for her gown, pulled it out and laid it on the bed. While she changed, Jesse ventured downstairs to see what bargain he could strike with his uncle.

"Why the shotgun weddin', boy? You get yourself into some trouble?" Welt jeered as Jesse descended the last step.

Jesse rolled his eyes, his lips pursed with terse irritation, "No, I did not get myself into any trouble, and it wasn't a shotgun wedding." It was times like these when Jesse wondered how Welt Everett could possibly be his mother's brother. His mother was so refined, kindhearted, and generous. Then again, Welt and his mother were only half-siblings. The difference in fathers must account for the contrast.

"I was just givin' ya a hard time, boy. No need in snippin' my head clean off!"

Jesse tried to soften his features. He had to get on his uncle's good side for this, and he'd already gotten off to a rotten start. Jesse forced a smile. "I know, I know... you love to tease."

"And I tease those I love," Welt added with a happy nod.

Jesse's smile grew a bit more genuine. "I was wondering if you might do me a bit of a favor. I'd like to take Jillian on a trip for a couple weeks and wondered if you'd mind watching the store while we're gone?"

"I suppose I could do that," his uncle pensively rubbed his whiskers. "Where're you takin' her?"

"It's a surprise," Jesse answered.

"For her or for me?" Welt chuckled.

Jesse did not reply but turned toward the steps, "Thanks, Uncle. We'll leave first thing in the morning. I appreciate your help." He started not to say anything about selling the store for now. It might be easier to only mention the trip and leave it at that. But, then again, maybe Welt needed some time to think on whether he'd want the store and to gather his funds.

Jesse stepped back toward his uncle, "Welt, you really love this store, don't you?"

"It's a fine store, yep. Why?" he eyed his nephew suspiciously. "What are you drivin' at?"

"Would you consider purchasing it back from me?"

"Buy it back?"

"You end up spending more time here than you do out fortune hunting, and I'm thinking of becoming a farmer and raising a family instead of working in this stuffy store. It's not all I thought it would be."

"A farmer? What do you know about farmin'?"

"I know enough, and Jillian knows much."

"She wants you to be a farmer? First day married and you're already givin' up all your dreams!" Welt snorted and shook his head disgustedly. "What a wimp you turned out to be."

Jesse gritted his teeth and forced himself to reply civilly, "Just think about it, Welt." He sighed. "I aim to sell the mercantile. If you want it, I'll give you first dibs. Just pay me what I paid you. With all the improvements I've made around here, that's quite a steal. But if you don't want it, let me know, and I'll find another buyer."

Without waiting for a reply, Jesse climbed the steps and ventured briskly down the narrow passageway. His blood pressure still boiled from his encounter with Welt. The old geezer knew which buttons to push to set Jesse off like a flint striking steel wool. When he reached his door, he realized what entering that room meant. Little had he known earlier that day that the woman he'd kissed at the falls would be waiting in his bed that evening! He took several deep breaths, and reached for the doorknob.

In her nightgown, she stood at the mirror brushing her long silky hair. When he entered, she turned toward him. Even though he tried to let it go and prepare to enjoy his wedding night, irritation still creased his brow and anger clenched his fists. She completed the stroke of her brush and set it on the dresser, her eyes riveted upon him.

"What happened?" she asked, knowing that his conversation with Welt had evidently not gone well.

"He's an irritating old mule," Jesse grumbled as he crossed to his closet and slipped off his coat, vest and shirt and hung them in his closet in their appropriate locations. Jillian's worried gaze followed him.

"What did he say?"

"He thinks I'm a fool to sell the store," he stewed as he sat on the edge of the bed, removed his shoes and then leaned forward to place them in the closet.

"Jesse," she approached him, standing directly in front of him so that he had to lift his eyes to meet hers. "I've been thinking. It's wrong of us to put you in a position where you're forced to sell the store. Right now you think you want to do this, but what if years from now you resent me for it? Resent my people for it?"

"I won't," he put his hands to her waist and tugged her closer.

"But how do you know? You've worked hard to obtain this mercantile, and then in a heartbeat you're asked to sell it and start over as a farmer. I've never even heard you say you wanted to be a farmer before today."

"Jillian," he rose to his feet, placing his palm to her cheek. "I want to do this. I don't enjoy running a store. I thought I would, but really what I'd like to do is" he hesitated, dropped his hand from her cheek, afraid to tell her what he really wanted to do.

"It's not farming, is it?" her palm compassionately stroked the bristles of his chiseled jaw.

"No," he sighed, a weak smile upturning his lips.

"Then what? Tell me," she prodded.

He sighed and then lifted his hopeful gaze toward her, "I like to build things, like my wagon and furniture. I did that in my father's store growing up, and my dad sold the things I made. Because I'd grown up working in the store, I thought it the best way to trade my wares, but I hate the management of it. I just want to build things."

"Then build things, Jesse! We can always find places to sell your creations. There's no point in you settling for being a farmer when there's something else you love doing."

He took her face in his strong, calloused hands. She understood now why they were calloused - from woodworking after store hours. "So you'll be all right with me being a craftsman instead of a farmer?"

"Of course!" she smiled. "I just want you to be happy. Just promise me one thing."

"What's that?"

"That the first thing you build for me is a house."

"Only if the second is a cradle," he winked, and then lifted her in his arms. In one powerful motion he set her gently in the center of his bed. Her heart throbbed wildly within her as his enthralling emerald eyes stole her breath. His strapping form hovered above her, and her hands caressed the muscles of his abdomen, finding their way along his chest and behind his neck. Every care, every worry, and fear he vanquished from her mind with the adoration in his eyes, the thrilling sensation of his touch, and the bewitching spell his lips wove upon the hollow of her throat. The realization that he was hers possessed her every thought, and her hands vanished into the lush thickness of his hair. Her head fell backwards into the pillow as his attentions to the sweet tenderness of her neck and shoulders increased. His kisses teased the corners of her mouth, her cheeks, her chin. Her heart screamed for the delicious taste of his lips, for their prior encounter at the waterfall had left her craving the rapturous intensity of his mouth worshiping hers.

Her hands slipped to his cheeks, and a sigh escaped her lungs as his lips finally found hers. He seemed unable to pull her close enough in his powerful enveloping arms, and his every tantalizing caress only heightened rather than quenched her thirst for his nearness. Of all the exchanges she'd transacted, Jillian knew that this night would be the most gratifying and exhilarating of all.

~*~

Jillian's arm rested on her sleeping husband's chest. Her chin leaning on her forearm, she watched him, memorizing every dimple, every fleck of gold in his brown hair, the way his wavy locks lay against his ears, the bristles of his mustache. Her fingertips traced the contours of his lips, still astonished by their softness. It was the first opportunity she'd had to observe him without his notice, and she felt like a child left home alone to sneak a peek inside her Christmas presents. The sun had already started to rise, casting orange, yellow, red and purple rays throughout the bedroom as it refracted through a crystal that hung in the window.

She hated to wake him. She'd rather lie there, feeling the rise and fall of his rhythmic breathing and the warmth of his skin next to hers. But they did need to leave. Her palm went to his cheek, gently caressing the morning bristles. His eyes stirred beneath their lids, his thick dark eyelashes fluttering. She leaned forward and kissed his lips softly. His parted, returning her affection. His hands went to her hips, pulling her to him and shifting her onto her back.

"We need to get ready to leave," she whispered as she looked up into his enticing emerald eyes.

"If you wished to lure me from my bed, wife, this is not the way to do it," his eyes twinkled.

"How should I have awakened you?"

"It's not so much what you should have done as much as what you should not have done."

"Which was?"

"First, if you wanted me to leave our bed, you would not have blessed me with one of your intoxicating kisses."

"So do not kiss you awake," her eyes made a gesture of mental notation.

"Right. Secondly, do not rest your body across mine," he added.

"Very well," she nodded, her eyes lit with mirth. "Anything else?"

"Yes, your attire… it should be," his hand caressed the length of her slender bronze arm, finally lacing her fingers through his.

"Very well," she smiled. "I'll wear a flour sack next time," she chuckled.

"It probably wouldn't help. Your beauty would radiate no matter your attire," he kissed her neck, lingering to inhale the sweet sent of her skin.

"I once heard tell of a woman who tossed a bucket of cold water on her man to wake him and swatted him with a frying pan when he misbehaved. Should I adopt her methods?" Jillian giggled.

"No, thank you, I'll take my chances with my beautiful bride draped over me, waking me with her affections."

"But we'll never accomplish anything that way," she chuckled.

"Perhaps a cradle," he answered with a mischievous twinkle in his eyes just before his lips met hers.

~*~

Jesse saddled and packed their horses for the trip. They were getting a later start of it than he had planned, but in the end he decided it would work out all right. While Jillian finished preparing breakfast, Welt sat at the table observing her work.

"So you've persuaded Jesse into becoming a farmer?" Welt needled.

Jillian raised her eyes toward him, "Jesse is free to do as he pleases, Mr. Everett."

"So you're saying that you had nothing to do with him giving up a store he's worked years to purchase?"

Jillian did not reply. She didn't trust the man, and in the last couple minutes, she'd decided she didn't like him very much either.

"Do I need to repeat my question, girl? You do speak English. I've heard ya. Do ya have trouble understandin' it suddenly, then?"

Jillian gritted her teeth, trying to contain the venomous reply that floated through her mind.

"Welt, I believe, if you want breakfast, you better leave my wife alone." Jesse entered the kitchen and stood over his uncle, his eyes blazing daggers at the old man.

"I'm not doin' a thing to your wife, boy, but I'd say she's done a thing or two to you! She's got ya so as ya can't even think clearly anymore!"

"Leave, Welt." Jesse pointed to the door.

"Ah, you wouldn't toss me out. You need me to cover your hind end at the store!"

"I'll board it up before I stand here and let you insult my wife. Better yet, I'll march right over to Art Higgins and sell it for what he offered me last month. You can be on your way." Jesse turned as if the conversation had ended, grabbed a piece of bacon and put his arm comfortingly around his wife's shoulder.

"You wouldn't sell it to Higgins! He's a no good, connivin' weasel!"

"I will if you can't have an ounce of respect and stay out of our business. It's none of my concern who takes the place, so long as I get my money out of it."

Welt reached into his pocket and pulled out a sack of gold Eagles. "There, take that and sign the store back over to me. You and your Cherokee half-breed can get on out of here. It's none of my concern whether you want to be a manure sloppin' farmer after you've worked so hard to be somethin' more!"

Jesse grabbed Jillian's hand and tugged her out of the kitchen, down the hallway, and up the stairs to his bedroom where he opened a drawer and pulled out his deed to the mercantile.

"Are you sure you really want to do this, Jesse?"

"What? Sell it to that worthless uncle of mine?"

"Sell it at all?" she replied.

"I want to sell it, Jillian. I want rid of it today!" he tugged her hand and led her back down the hallway toward the kitchen.

Welt still sat leaning back in his chair, now with his legs crossed and his boots propped up on the kitchen table. Jesse took a quill, signed the paper and flung it at his uncle, grabbed the bag of gold from the table, counted it and shoved it in his pocket. Welt rose and started for the door and into the hallway.

"Wrap up that breakfast, Jillian. I'll get my belongings, and we'll eat on the way," Jesse ordered and stomped from the room, passing Welt in the hallway. Jillian stood, somewhat astonished at her husband's decisive behavior. Welt hovered just outside the kitchen door, shaking his head and grumbling, "Like a pup on a leash. 'Tis why I never married, it is. May as well be a pup on a leash." The old man reentered the kitchen, grabbed a piece of bacon from the counter and ate it.

"Think not that he'll be happy as a farmer, girl! More'n likely he'll use ya, take ya for your Indian treasure, and toss ya aside once ya've served his needs. At least that's what I'd be doin'." Without another word, he stomped out of the room and into the mercantile.

Jillian could feel the hot stinging tears well behind her eyelids. Even if it wasn't true, it still hurt. It was as if the old man knew the exact location of Running Deer's remnant thorn and shoved it further into the fleshy softness of her heart.

Chapter Seven

Jesse decided they would make better time on horseback. As he rode alongside his bride, he couldn't help watching her. Something about how she moved, the angelic grace and charm with which she made even the simplest of movements mesmerized him. An exhilarating mystery was this enchantress. He loved her with every ounce of his soul, yet he had to admit that he actually knew very little about her. He craved her nearness. She constantly dominated his thoughts, distracting him, capturing his every waking moment and many of his sleeping ones. To touch her, hold her, inhale the sweet softness of her skin was to taste heaven upon earth. A single glance from her and all of his defenses tumbled. She instinctively lured him as if he were but a bee drawn to the sweet nectar of an intoxicatingly vibrant wild flower that remained oblivious to its power of attraction.

But there was more to their relationship than this ethereal tether connecting them. What he did know of her swelled his heart with love. Her courage in the face of danger had garnered his attentions first. He'd never seen a woman stand so calm and resolute before the likes of Chet LaSalle. The man embodied the word foul, reeked of every vice, and exuded the essence of lasciviousness and trifling greed. Yet, Jillian hadn't so much as flinched as the man harassed her that first day at the mercantile. Her cinnamon eyes had flashed daring determination as if to convey the resolution that she'd fight to the death before the varmint would rob her of what she held most dear.

The compassionate grace with which she served the elderly and the needy could not help but win his heart. Never was there a condescending tone or manner in her interactions with them, rather a respect, almost a reverence shone from her countenance.

While his uncle had transacted business with her prior to Jesse's arrival and commented on her savvy bartering skills, Jesse had to admit that she molded like putty in his own hands: her thoughts and intentions as transparent as glass. Then again, perhaps it was he who sculpted like clay to the formation of her desires. Maybe she simply permitted him to believe it was he who wanted to exchange excessive amounts of merchandise for a simple afternoon in her presence. Yes, perhaps she was a shrewder trader than he'd given her credit for. She did always manage to walk away from any barter with a rich amount of tangible goods.

But who really had the better bargain? For he would trade every ounce of gold he owned to call the breathtaking angel his own. And now she was, yet still he knew so little about her. Would she truly be his until he became intimately aware of every corner of her soul? What were her deepest desires? Her most haunting fears? He'd seen her strengths, what of her weaknesses? How could he fully protect and provide for her until he knew such things?

Then there were the everyday details that most people learn of each other. What had she been like as a child? Did she enjoy reading, if so what books entertained her most? Could she sew, paint, or sculpt? What made her laugh out loud? What brought sentimental tears to her eyes? These questions tugged the corners of his mind, begging answers.

He stared at her with smiling eyes, yet his lips held the expression of a man lost in thought.

"What are your thoughts just now?" she inquired.

"Hmm?" he startled slightly, awakened from his reverie. "You," he replied.

"How do you do that?" she asked.

"A better question would be 'How do I not think of you?'" a smile now upturned his lips.

"No," she chuckled and pulled the reins of her horse sidestepping closer to Jesse's. "How do you smile with your eyes yet keep your lips so serious?"

He raised a questioning eyebrow, "I didn't realize I did."

"Then tell me, love, what were you thinking just now?"

"As I said, only of you."

"What about me?" she pressed.

"How much I love you," he caressed her cheek with his palm, and her face owned a radiant smile. How he loved her smile! It contained more loveliness than a thousand flowers.

"Is that all? There was a somberness to your expression."

He remained quiet for a moment, grasping for a way to convey his thoughts succinctly. "There's so much I don't know about you."

"What would you like to know?"

"I'm not sure where to begin."

"Just ask," she prompted.

"What do you enjoy doing? Do you sew, paint, sculpt? Anything of the like?"

"Music. I play the flute."

"You do? Did you bring it with you?"

"It's in my bag."

"In here?" he pointed to her saddlebag as they continued to ride alongside one another.

"I believe so," she nodded.

Jesse pulled his horse to a stop, and she halted hers.

"You want me to play it now?" she asked with surprise.

"Please," he encouraged as he unbuckled her saddlebag and began rummaging. He handed her the handcrafted wooden flute and gestured for her to play. He held her horse's reins with his so she could use both hands to play as they continued their journey. The birds chirped in harmony as the haunting hollow tones of the Cherokee flute echoed off the hills. It was as if the ghosts of a hundred generations sent their stories through the melody of Jillian's flute. Jesse recognized the song as one he'd heard in the village the night Joe Vann made his exodus from Spring Place. The mournful Cherokee melody squeezed a single tear from Jillian's eye, streaming down her cheek, and for some reason he could not explain, moisture brimmed in his own.

He proudly complimented her upon the song's completion and encouraged her to continue playing. She did so for some time, entertaining them as they traveled through the lush green landscape of the northwest Georgia hills and into Tennessee.

They traveled all day and into the evening, taking turns asking each other questions and acquainting themselves with the person to whom they had pledged their love and devotion. Finally stopping to build camp for the night, Jesse built a fire, and Jillian prepared their meal. After unloading and watering the horses, Jesse sat down on the ground and leaned against a log by the fire as Jillian finished cooking.

He crossed one ankle over the other and put his hands behind his head, "What is your sweetest memory?" he asked.

She thought for a moment and then answered, "I would say that years hence, I would remember the past day as my fondest memory." She smiled as she prepared two plates of food.

"And your greatest fear?" he asked.

"My greatest fear?" her brow furrowed. She started to say snakes, but Running Deer's warning intruded upon her thoughts, and she decided that her worst fear would be that Running Deer was right about her husband… that he didn't really love her but only pretended to for the treasure. She shook her head in frustration in an attempt to drive away the traitorous thought. She had no reason to doubt him. She never read anything but love and devotion in his eyes. Surely a man could not elicit such cherished emotions within her if his feelings for her were not genuine.

Noting her conflicted expression, Jesse sat upright. She shrugged and returned to the meal attempting to avoid answering the question.

"Come now. How can I be there to protect you against it if I don't know what it is?" he pleaded.

"Snakes," she grimaced. "I loathe them."

He stood up and approached her from behind, slipping his arms about her waist and kissing her cheek. "Then stay close to me. I'll be your personal serpent slayer." She thanked him with a pleased turn of her lips, handed him his plate, and they sat down together.

"What is your sweetest memory?" she inquired.

"I think it's that first day we went for a stroll, and I saw you coming toward me with the silver comb in your hair. I knew that day that you'd be mine."

"Oh, you did, did you? Rather presumptuous of you, was it not?" she teased. "And, what if I had not wanted to be yours?"

"I'd been forced to spirit you away and convince you that you should love me, too," he winked.

"Indeed?" she laughed aloud, "You strike me not as the kidnapping kind."

"Oh, desperate men do desperate things," he chuckled.

"And your deepest fear?" she inquired.

He thought for a moment and then somberly shook his head negatively.

"Now, I told you mine," she coaxed, "You must share yours."

He took a deep breath and with his penetrating emerald eyes locked with hers, he replied, "That you'd ever stop loving me."

She set her plate aside and placed her slender fingers to his bristled cheek, "Your fears are unfounded, my love, for it can never be." She leaned forward and pressed a gentle kiss to his lips. He abandoned his own dinner to the ground beside him and pulled her onto his lap, one arm about her back and the other lost in her silky ebony tresses, supporting her neck with his palm. With every new insight he'd gained that day, he had dreamt of this moment when he could hold her in his arms once more and love her completely, thoroughly, for the intimate bonds had grown stronger with the day's passing. He remembered thinking the night before that he could not love her more, but he had been wrong.

The light-headed delirium of his tantalizing kisses sent her senses reeling, and she completely lost herself in her husband's affections. Gone was all trace of doubt and uncertainty. If Running Deer's thorn remained, then surely Jesse would remove all afflicting remnants of it with his gentle touch, loving words, and rapt attention to her every need. Just as every last thought swept from her mind, a twig broke in the distance. A horse whinnied, and Jillian's startled hands went to Jesse's chest, pushing him back.

"What was that?" she asked, and he, with slightly greater difficulty, pulled his mind from his amorous objectives. He sat upright, lifting her with him.

Again another breaking twig sent the hair rising on the back of Jillian's neck. "Someone's followed us!" she whispered, and slid from his lap, crouching low to the ground. Jesse slowly reached for his rifle, rose to his feet and carefully stepped toward the darkness.

"Who's out there?" he shouted. "Show yourself, you coward!"

Silence. Nothing but crickets' song and bullfrog moans.

"Who are you? What do you want?" Jesse called once more.

Silence and then another horse whinny and galloping hoof beats followed and faded into the distance. Jillian came to stand behind her husband, placing a hand to his shoulder.

"Perhaps there is one thing that frightens me more than snakes," she mumbled.

He put his arms around her, pulling her into his protective embrace.

~*~

Even after daybreak, Jillian could not shake the threatening sensation that they were being followed. Occasionally she stopped her horse, turned it suddenly and peered in the direction of a stray sound. It would either be a deer, a rabbit or nothing visible. A known villain she could deal with, but a lurking, faceless menace that might attack as they slept or ambush by day set her nerves frightfully on edge. Jesse too felt an eerie foreboding, but refused to voice it to his wife. Instead he continued to calm and reassure her by day and to hold her protectively in his embrace by night, his rifle always at the ready.

It was nearly nightfall when they reached the home of Jillian's grandparents - a modest home, spanned by a welcoming front porch. Matching rocking chairs stood guard on either side of the entrance. An aged man perched in one of them swaying back and forth as he carved a figure from a block of wood. He continued to rock as his eyes looked up in the direction of the sound of hoof beats.

"Emma!" he hollered. "We've got comp'ny!"

The couple dismounted their horses and led them toward the porch to tie the reins. Just then, a silvery-haired woman with a merry smile exited the home. The only wrinkles upon her lovely face were those created by a lifetime of laughter and joy found in everyday living.

"My, my! Is it who I think it is?" she called, placing her aged hand dramatically to her bosom.

"Grandma!" Jillian nodded affirmatively.

"Who is it, Emma?" the gentleman called. Jillian stepped briskly onto the porch and embraced her grandmother heartily.

"Oh, you're just so beautiful! You've gotten so tall!" the woman cooed over Jillian, placing her hands to Jillian's cheeks with a loving squeeze.

"Well, who in tar nation is it, Emma?" the gentleman's voice grew more exasperated.

"Why Homer, it's Jillian - our little Jillian!"

Jillian turned to her grandfather who seemed to be staring in her direction yet without recognition.

"Your poor ol' Grandpa can't see too well anymore, I'm afraid." She lowered her voice to a whisper, "And his hearin' ain't too good either."

"What? What did you say, Emma?" he asked, "Did you say Jillian?"

Jillian crossed to where her grandfather still sat in the rocker, and he braced his hands on the arms, pushing himself to a standing position and outstretched his arms. Jillian fell into his loving embrace.

"Grandpa, it's so good to see you again," she looked up into his face, and it appeared as if he could discern her appearance to some degree at the closer proximity. He clasped his cold hands to her cheeks and cried, "Oh, my sweet Jillie girl!" Kissing her firmly on her cheek, he held her so tightly that she wondered whether he'd spend the last of his waning strength on the affection.

"And who have we here?" Emma put out her hand, motioning Jesse to ascend the porch steps and join them.

Jillian turned toward her grandmother, one arm still around her grandfather's waist. She extended her hand to Jesse. "Grandma, Grandpa, this is my husband, Jesse Whitmore."

"Your husband!" Emma gasped, another astonished palm flung to her bosom.

"Why you're too young to be married, Jillie girl! You're only, what - fourteen, fifteen?"

Jillian chuckled, "No grandpa, I'm twenty. Almost twenty-one!"

"No!" his voice lowered in denial. "Wasn't but yesterday you were runnin' pigtail 'cross the fields chasin' bunny rabbits with your brother John with little Lizzy shadowin' behind!"

"How are John and Elizabeth?" Emma interjected. "How is everyone?"

Emma motioned for the group to go inside where Jillian answered questions about her family, explained their current situation to her grandparents, and asked for the name of the man selling the property they had come to purchase.

"Lamont Fields is his name," Emma replied.

"Works over at the livery in town," Homer added.

"A nice man... a very nice man," Emma cooed.

"Honest as the day is long. Now there's a man you can trust, Jillie girl," Homer interjected. Jesse couldn't help but smile every time Homer referred to his bride as "Jillie girl." The term of endearment sent his mind to imagining the little ebony haired child scampering through meadows, chasing rabbits, hiding from her brother in cornfields, and begging her mother for bandages for her skinned knees. He wished he had more time to spend with Jillian's grandparents to learn about her childhood escapades. But Jillian and he would be back soon, and then he could sit for hours and listen to Homer and Emma's tales of years gone by.

They spent an enjoyable evening with Jillian's grandparents. Homer played the fiddle, and Jesse coaxed Jillian onto her flute. In singing along with Homer's fiddle, Jillian learned that her husband owned a rich, melodious tenor voice. Finally, their evening festivities ended and Emma went to prepare the spare room for their guests. Jillian stepped outside into the evening air, which had cooled significantly from the sweltering day.

"Feels heavenly out here, doesn't it?" Jesse noted, slipping an arm around her shoulders.

"Heaven it is," she agreed.

"I like your grandparents," Jesse smiled.

"They are quite the entertaining pair, are they not?" Jillian giggled.

"Yes, Jillie girl, they are," he teased.

"Oh, now don't start with that! I'm too old for that Jillie girl nonsense!"

Jesse turned her toward him, curled his forefinger under her chin and lifted her gaze to his. With a teasing smile he winked, "I suppose you're right... that girl has grown into a beautiful woman... no, I correct myself... an enchanting angel."

~*~

When they arrived at the trading post early the next morning, Jillian and Jesse dismounted their horses outside the livery, and Jesse took his wife's hand. They stepped into the establishment where they found a burly man, his sleeves rolled up to the middle of his biceps, shoeing a horse.

"We were told that a Lamont Fields worked here at the livery and has some land for sale?" Jesse inquired.

"Yes, he does work here. Owns the place, he does."

"May I speak with him?" Jesse inquired.

"Yes, you may," the man replied and continued to shoe the horse.

Jesse looked around the establishment searching for anyone else who could be the man they sought. "When might we speak with him?"

"You are speaking with him," the man's eye darted up from his work with a mirthful twinkle.

Jesse chortled slightly and began, "I'm Jesse Whitmore, and this is my wife, Jillian. We came to see if your land's still for sale - the five hundred acres?"

"Yes, it is."

"I'd like to purchase it."

"And you know the price?"

Jesse handed the man a parchment that Jillian's grandparents had given him concerning the property, "I assume the price is as it states here?"

"Yes," the man nodded.

"Then we'd like to buy it."

"Have you even seen it?" the man inquired.

"My wife's grandparents told us about it, and they recommended it. That's good enough for us."

"Who are your grandparents, Mrs. Whitmore?"

Jillian replied, "Homer and Emma Pierce."

"Oh, yes, I know them well," the man dropped his work, wiped his hands on his handkerchief and jovially shook both their hands.

"We know you're a busy man, Mr. Fields. We'd love to see it, but didn't know if you had the time to show it to us."

"You have the money to pay with you?" the man inquired.

"Yes," Jesse replied.

"Then I have the time. Let me lock up, grab the deed, and we'll go now."

Jesse and Jillian accompanied Mr. Fields to a lovely piece of property, just as Sophia's parents had described. It was well irrigated with streams and ponds and nestled in a valley of lush foliage and long stretches of flat farmland. Rather than use all the gold Jillian had brought, Jesse decided it might be less traceable to the Cherokees if they used a combination of nuggets and the gold Eagles he'd received from his uncle Welt.

The plan worked well, and Mr. Fields did not question where they had obtained the gold but simply signed over the deed, pleased to have made the transaction. After Mr. Fields left, Jesse and Jillian examined the property and decided on a beautiful knoll upon which to build their farmhouse. After spending lunch on the site and discussing their plans for their new home, they began their journey back to Georgia.

Jillian noted that the eerie feeling of being watched seemed to pass, and the remainder of the trip concluded without event. Soon they were back at the mercantile retrieving Jesse's wagon to help the villagers with their move.

Chapter Eight

Sophia Elliott swept the front porch of her log home for the last time as Jesse helped John load the last of their belongings into the wagons. It was the house John had built soon after their marriage. Their children had been born there, raised there and played within its walls. So many cherished memories echoed within the walls of the cozy home, and she could not restrain the tears that spilled freely upon her cheeks.

"It will be all right, Mama," Jillian took her mother into a comforting embrace. "You'll love the new place. It's a lovely piece of property."

"But we'll have to start over from scratch," Sophia brushed away a tear in frustration.

"Just think about it, Mama," Elizabeth joined in as she pointed toward the house. "You never liked the absence of a window in the kitchen. And the stairs are too narrow."

"We almost bump our heads every time we ascend them," Jillian added.

"You always wanted a bigger bedroom," Elizabeth continued.

"Pa and Jesse can build you exactly what you want this time," Jillian embraced her mother's shoulders.

"You're right, you're both absolutely right," Sophia nodded and carried her broom inside to the fireplace. "We'll burn it for luck - for better times in our new home," Sophia said as she broke the broom over her knee and tossed it into the fireplace. The three of them stood before the flame watching the broom blaze and the bristles sputter and shrivel to fine wispy black hairs and vanish into smoke.

"Are you ready then?" John asked as he stepped into the doorway. The two younger children, Polly and Pierce, scurried past him, out the door and toward Jesse's wagon.

Just as they shut the door behind them, Martha's husband ran across the yard. "The baby, the baby's coming! She's calling for you, Jillian," he panted as he came to stand before Jillian.

"Now?" Jesse asked in surprise.

"Oh, my!" Sophia exclaimed. "But we're running out of time."

"Mama, Papa, will you please take the children in your wagon? Jesse and I better stay behind with his. Martha and the baby will need something more protective to transport them for the journey."

"Yes, an excellent idea," Sophia nodded in agreement.

"But we can't all fit in Pa's wagon," Elizabeth noted.

"Elizabeth, why don't you stay with us and help with the delivery?" Jillian suggested.

Elizabeth crinkled her nose. Watching a birth wasn't one of her favorite activities. Blood made her squeamish.

"Don't worry, Elizabeth," Jillian put an arm around her sister's shoulder. "I'll warn you in time so you won't have to watch the actual birth. You can keep Henry company."

"Please, come quickly!" Martha's husband, Henry, tugged at her sleeve.

"Jesse, please finish up here. Elizabeth, come with me," Jillian took Elizabeth's hand and the pair lifted their skirts and hurried along after Henry.

"But I wanted to ride in Jesse's wagon!" eight-year-old Pierce whined.

"We'll catch up with you soon, and then I promise you can ride with me in the front of the wagon," Jesse consoled the boy as he lifted him from the front seat and set him on the ground.

"We'll travel the way we planned, and you and the girls catch up with us as soon as you can," John extended his hand to Jesse in a firm handshake, and the family was on its way.

When Jesse reached Martha's house, he could hear the painful moans of the mother inside. He winced at the thought of the torment a woman must go through bearing children. A nervous fear swept over him as he thought of Jillian enduring such agony. This was a part of the process he hadn't spent much time considering.

Again, Martha's cry rent the air, and Henry hurriedly stepped out on the front porch.

"Not a place for men, I suppose?" Jesse smiled at the soon-to-be-father.

"I wanted to stay, but Jillian threw me out."

"My Jillian threw you out?" Jesse chuckled incredulously. To say the man was large would have been an understatement. He stood nearly as tall as Joe Vann.

"She's feisty when she means business," Henry rubbed his arm where Jillian had pinched it to persuade him to exit.

"Why didn't she want you in there?" Jesse asked, peaking inside the door to observe his wife busily working over Martha and giving Elizabeth orders about what items to prepare.

"She said I was in the way," Henry muttered.

An hour passed as the two men sat out on the front porch and waited. Elizabeth stepped outside.

"Is the baby here?" Henry asked anxiously.

"No, it will be some time still," Elizabeth shrugged. "I just need some air. I think I'll walk for a spell. Martha's asking for you, Henry. Go to her."

Henry protectively rubbed the smart from where Jillian had pinched the back of his arm above his elbow.

Noting his movement, Elizabeth chuckled, "Don't worry, Jillian said it would be fine. She told me to get you." Henry started into the house, and Jesse followed him to see if he could be of assistance.

"Tell Jillian I'll be back in a few minutes. I need to stretch my legs and catch my breath," Elizabeth said as she stepped off the porch and started toward the field.

"Very well," Henry nodded and the men disappeared into the house.

Tense panic froze every muscle in Elizabeth's body, and then with all her energy, she fought her assailant. Something gagged her mouth, and a blanket draped over her head. She couldn't see! Strong arms held her hands behind her back and bound her feet. She could feel taut scratchy ropes being brutally tied to her hands, arms, and feet. Violently she attempted to fight her assailants, but the bonds were too tight and her resistance only served to grind the ropes, cutting into her flesh. She tried to scream, but only muffled sounds could be discerned through the gag wrapped around her mouth. She panicked, she couldn't swallow, and the horrid feeling that she might suffocate from the constricting cloth filled her heart with terror!

Tears streamed from her eyes. Inhaling deeply through her nose, she attempted to control her emotions. The last thing she needed to do was burst into uncontrollable sobs. She'd suffocate for sure if her nose became blocked. She felt her body slammed forward to the earth, and she ached from the sudden unprotected jolt to her chest. Someone yanked her braids, pulling her head backward and sawed away at her locks. Just as it cut through, her head released and slammed to the earth. A sickening wave swept over her, and instantly she lost consciousness.

"Go get Elizabeth, please, Jesse!" Jillian motioned for the door. "I need her help here."

Jesse nodded, stepped outside the house, and searched the horizon for his sister-in-law. When he couldn't find her, he went around to the back of the cabin, and his eyes surveyed the fields. Nothing but corn. He yelled her name, hoping she'd hear him and return to the house.

No reply. No sign of her. Just as he turned back toward the house to see if she might have gone in a different direction, he noticed a knife stabbed to the outer wall.

From it hung a leather bag, a braided lock of jet black hair, and a parchment waving in the breeze beneath the blade's tip. Jesse's breath caught and a terrible foreboding filled his chest. He hurried to the spot and read the note.

If you want to see your sister alive again, you'll fill this bag with gold and come to the weeping willow at the burial grounds. Be there at sunset. Attempt to track us before then, and she'll die a horrible death.

Jesse pulled the lock of hair, the bag, and knife from the wall and carried them along with the parchment inside the house.

"Did you get Elizabeth?" Jillian asked, without lifting her eyes from her suffering friend.

"She - She's been taken," Jesse stammered and held up the articles as proof.

"What?" Jillian cried as she came to stand before her husband and examined the items he held. Her hands went to her cheeks in horror, and tears spilled from her eyes. "Oh, Jesse, what have I done? What have I done?" She clutched her throat to ease the horrible pain there.

Jesse took her shoulders in his firm grip, "You didn't do anything, Jillian. This isn't your fault."

"I made her stay. She should be riding with everyone else, not here unprotected! I should never have asked her to stay!" She was on the brink of hysterics. Jesse had never seen her so distraught.

"Jillian, honey, get a hold of yourself. We've got to act quickly. Where is the gold?"

"What?" her eyes narrowed suspiciously.

"They want the gold," he held up the bag. "We have to fill it with gold so we can save Elizabeth."

The trauma of the situation seemed to be taking its toll on Martha, and the tension increased the pains of her labor. As she cried out, her husband clutched her hand and comfortingly held a wet cloth to her brow.

Jillian's attention turned back to her friend. As she rushed to her side, she told Jesse, "Let me finish here, and then I'll go get it."

"No, Jillian," Jesse pulled his pocket watch out to read the time. "We've only three hours before sunset. Tell me where it is, and I'll go get it while you tend to Martha."

Jillian's confused expression went from her husband to Martha and back.

"We don't have time for you to do both, and you can't leave Martha now," he insisted, staring at her as if she had lost her senses.

Jillian suddenly grabbed her husband's arm, led him into a second bedroom and shut the door. He stared at her expectantly waiting for her to tell him where the treasure was so they could save Elizabeth.

"I - I can't," her eyes brimmed with tears, and she turned from him.

"Jillian, what's more important - Elizabeth's life or lifeless chunks of metal?" he was becoming exasperated. She didn't answer, but simply held her hands to her cheeks, torn by the weight of the decision placed before her. There was Martha and the baby to think about. She certainly couldn't leave them now. Then there was her beloved sister whom she'd willingly trade places with at this moment, and then there was her loyalty to the clan and her duty to protect the treasure - a treasure she wasn't even supposed to know about! Why did Jesse even think she knew of its location? Was he behind all of this? Had he and his uncle concocted this plan to steal the treasure and abduct her sister? What had Running Deer done to her? Why did he have to make her doubt her husband like this?

"Why do you hesitate?" Jesse's hands went to her shoulders, and she shrugged him off and stepped further away. Suddenly it all became crystal clear to him, and Jesse felt as if someone had slugged him in the stomach, knocking the wind out of him. "You don't trust me," he whispered. "You think I'm behind this!"

The horror of what her doubt and fear had done to them squeezed Jillian's throat like a vice and fresh tears escaped her eyes. She shook her head negatively, "No, no, I don't think that." Jesse threw the bag to the floor and grabbed Jillian's shoulders, forcing her to turn and face him.

"Then look in my eyes, and tell me you trust me to get the gold and save your sister." He could see the doubt, indecision, and pain in her countenance.

"I - I trust you to get the gold and save Elizabeth," she forced the words, wanting them desperately to be true. They had to be true! She couldn't - wouldn't believe her husband capable of the cruelty necessary to concoct such a plan. At that moment, Martha called out Jillian's name, begging her to return to her.

Jillian glanced toward the door and back at Jesse who still held her firmly by the shoulders. "It's behind our waterfall. There's a cave. There's a box of flints at the mouth of the cave so you can light a torch. Go back in there about a hundred feet, and you'll find the treasure. Fill the bag and leave the rest."

"Leave the rest!" he huffed angrily. "You don't trust me a bit, do you? Why would I take more than was necessary?"

"Jesse, of course I trust you. I just meant it needs to stay there."

He didn't believe her. He felt it deep in his bones. She didn't trust him! How could she think him capable of such dishonesty and greed? Did their time together mean nothing to her? Couldn't she read him as well as he could her? In frustration, he released her, bent over and angrily snatched the bag from the floor and stomped toward the door.

Jillian's heart ached so painfully that she felt her chest might explode. What had she done? He'd never given her cause to mistrust him, yet that was her first reaction - to assume he was involved. Just as he reached for the doorknob, she rushed to him and pulled his arm, turning him around.

"Jesse, don't leave like this," she pleaded.

"I have to leave for Elizabeth's sake," his fiery eyes blazed indignantly.

"Please, Jesse, I'm sorry," she put her hands around his neck and pulled his face toward hers, capturing his mouth with her own. He didn't respond, just stood there stoically uninvolved in her advances. But she did not relent. She kept kissing him, pleading with him to believe she trusted him, that she loved him and that she knew he would return to help Elizabeth.

His mind swirled with emotions. Anger and betrayal made strange bedfellows with love. The conflicting partners raged war inside him. Finally, he took her chin in his hand and let the anger and hurt pour out in a driven, emblazoned exchange. He kissed her long, hard, and relentlessly until the love and compassion warmed the icy chambers of his heart and gave way to a tender, softened kiss.

He broke from her, opened the door and strode out, "We'll talk about this later, Jillian. Tend to Martha, and I'll tend to Elizabeth." Then he was gone, out the door, and she prayed he'd be back.

Jesse released his fastest horse from the team that pulled his wagon, climbed on its back and charged toward the waterfall. The horse's nostrils flared and chugged the humid late summer air like a steam engine. Never slowing his pace, Jesse finally arrived at the lake. Quickly he stripped off his shirt and pants and dove into the water carrying the leather bag with him. He couldn't help but think of Jillian and the moments they'd spent there together - their wedding day it turned out to be.

As he climbed up on a rock by the waterfall, he remembered how she looked with the water streaming over her, how he'd wanted to hold her and how incredibly difficult it had been for him to put her away from him. He realized now that she'd been there that day to retrieve the gold for the land. She'd hidden the fact well, but he'd known the night he'd found her in the darkness of her parents' kitchen that she'd lied when she said she didn't know where the treasure was.

How could he read her so well and yet she should be so oblivious to his character? Why couldn't she trust him? These were the thoughts that plagued him as he stepped into the cave, lit a torch with the flints and ventured back into the cavern.

When his eyes met the gleaming display of precious metals, he released an audible gasp. He'd had no idea that there was this much gold and silver hidden! He'd expected a couple buckets, not gold bars the length of a child or heaping baskets of gold nuggets, coins and silver. Stunned, he slowly approached a bucket of gold nuggets and began scooping the metal into the leather bag until he'd filled it completely.

No wonder Jillian had been so protective of the stash! It would take a strong man to resist the temptation that this treasury provided. When he'd filled the bag, he tied the laces at the top and threw it over his shoulder and returned to the mouth of the cave. He extinguished the flame and stepped back into the water. The bag was heavy, making it a bit awkward to swim back to shore. But he did so quickly, dressed and put the gold in his saddlebag.

He rode at top speed to the burial grounds on the other side of the village, his mind whirling upon a way he could save Elizabeth and retrieve the gold for Jillian's people. If he brought back the gold, then she'd know she could trust him. He'd prove to her that he wasn't like the rest!

Elizabeth regained consciousness only to find herself still bound, gagged, and blindfolded. She didn't know with whom or where she was. She distinguished the voices of two separate men, but neither sounded familiar. She could overhear them discussing a ransom and where they would leave her. All she could do was hope and pray that Jillian knew the location of the gold or could reach someone who did in time to save her!

Jesse arrived at the burial ground near sunset. He dismounted his horse as he approached the weeping willow. To its trunk, a blade stabbed a piece of parchment. He pulled the paper from the tree.

Leave the gold here and go two hundred feet west to retrieve the girl. Try anything, and we'll kill you both.

Jesse pulled the bag of gold from his saddlebag and placed it at the foot of the tree, mounted his horse and galloped west toward the forest. There he found Elizabeth bound to a tree, still blindfolded and gagged.

"Elizabeth? Are you harmed?" he asked as he dismounted his horse, ran to his sister-in-law and pulled the flour sack from her face. Her grateful eyes were filled with relief as tears spilled onto her already tear-stained cheeks. Quickly he removed the cloth from her mouth.

"Oh, thank you, thank you, Mr. Whitmore."

"Now, you call me Jesse. We're family now," he answered as he continued to untie her from the tree.

"Your wrists look so sore. You put up quite a struggle. You've a bruise here on your forehead, too," he noted with concern. "Are you harmed anywhere else?"

"No, I don't think so."

"Did they... did they do anything else to you?" Jesse asked hesitantly, unable to voice the ugly possibilities of what such vile men might do to a lovely young maiden.

"No, no, just pushed me around a bit."

Jesse released a relieved sigh, "Good, good." He took her arm and led her to his horse, and assisted her in climbing into the saddle. "I want you to ride as fast as you can to Martha's. Jillian is still there helping with the baby. If the baby's born, tell Jillian to pack everyone up and leave immediately to join the others."

"Where are you going?" she asked Jesse as he turned back toward the burial ground.

"I'm going to get the gold back for the clan."

"Oh, no, Mr. Whitmore. Don't do that. It's not safe."

He turned back toward his sister-in-law, "She doesn't trust me, Elizabeth. I can't live knowing that my own wife doesn't trust me; and I love her too much to lose her. If I bring back the gold, she'll know she need not doubt me."

"She trusts you. You mustn't put your life in danger," Elizabeth pleaded.

"They're getting away. I have to go," he said as he slapped the rear of the horse, and it bolted forward. Her heart racing and her palms perspiring, Elizabeth determined she'd return for Henry's help before Jesse got himself killed.

Jesse hurried back to the burial grounds. He expected the villains to have ridden away, and he only realized after he'd sent Elizabeth off with his horse that if they had, he'd have no means of keeping up with them. Much to his surprise, the two men still stood by the weeping willow greedily running their grimy fingers through the nuggets and laughing over their good fortune. As Jesse drew closer, he recognized the two men and cocked his pistol. A sense of relief washed over him when he saw that it was Chet and his brother Chester LaSalle from the trading post. At least his uncle had no part in the kidnapping. He'd been afraid to find Welt behind all of this.

Quietly, he snuck up behind them, "Put it all back in the bag, boys, and hand it over."

Chet and Chester quickly turned their heads toward Jesse's voice. "You ain't expecting us to cut you in on the deal now, Whitmore?" Chet laughed his usual sickening drunken laugh that jiggled his immense belly, causing his saggy flesh to seep out from under his grimy shirt.

"That gold doesn't belong to you. Hand it over. I aim to give it back to its rightful owners," Jesse demanded in his most threatening voice, but inside he could feel his heart hammering the walls of his chest.

"Ah, you wouldn't shoot us. You're bluffin', city boy," Chet sneered.

Jesse fired a shot, hitting Chet's hat and sending it sailing from his head.

"I mean business, Chet. Toss your guns over here along with the gold; then get on your horses and ride away."

"See if I ever shop in your store again, Whitmore!" Chester muttered.

"Yeah, like that's gonna hurt him when he has all the gold," Chet grumbled, rolling his eyes and flicking his brother on the head with the back of his hand.

"Now!" Jesse demanded, and just as Chester tossed his gun toward Jesse's feet, Chet whipped his from his holster and fired, hitting Jesse in the left arm. The jolt sent Jesse's body backwards, and he returned fire, shooting twice in succession and hitting Chet in the heart. The earth seemed to rumble as Chet's immense body fell on his backside, and Chester ran to his brother.

"You've killed him!" Chester cried.

"And you'll be next if you don't toss that gold over here," Jesse barked as he squatted down. Blood drizzled down his arm onto his hand, dripping onto Chester's gun as he lifted the pistol, still aiming his own at the man.

Chester's expression hardened and intense hatred flickered in his eyes. He reached for the gold, making to toss it toward Jesse when instead he reached for a second pistol strapped to his boot. Just as he aimed it, Jesse heard a shot fire, sending Chester to his side beside his brother. Jesse stared at his gun. He didn't remember pulling the trigger. Looking behind him, he saw Welt, his smoking rifle still aimed at the villain.

"Welt?" Jesse's mouth dropped in amazement.

"I overheard 'em plannin' outside the store," Welt explained.

Jesse's eyes went from his uncle to the fallen men and back again. Slowly he and his uncle approached the brothers' bodies. Feeling their necks for a pulse, Welt affirmed that they'd both expired.

"I owe you my life, Welt," Jesse extended his hand to his uncle. Welt took it and pulled his nephew toward him, embracing him carefully so as not to cause further pain to Jesse's wounded arm.

"Think nothin' of it, boy," Welt released Jesse and reached down to lift the sack of gold. Handing it to Jesse, he said, "Here, I believe this belongs to your in-laws."

"Thanks," Jesse nodded. He looked back down at the men, "Do you think they were the ones who killed Running Deer and threatened the village?"

"Nope," Welt shook his head negatively. "That was the Bishop brothers – the ones who won the Cherokee land in the lottery. When the villagers refused to leave, they decided to take matters into their own hands. You need to get those people out of here before they return. Take my horse, and I'll clean up this mess," Welt offered.

"Are you sure?" Jesse asked.

"Yeah, you go on and catch up with the others and have someone take a look at that arm," Welt tied his handkerchief around Jesse's left arm to stop the bleeding. "I'll deal with any questions that may arise here."

Jesse extended his hand to his uncle once more, "I'm sorry for our differences, Uncle."

"Ah, get on out o' here before I change my mind and take a handful o' that gold for my trouble!" Welt smiled, slapping Jesse on his good shoulder.

Jesse returned a grateful smile and quickly strapped the gold into Welt's saddlebag and climbed onto the horse. He rode as fast as he could back toward Martha's house. On his way he met Henry, who had set out after him.

"You're injured," Henry pointed to Jesse's arm as his horse fell into step with Jesse's.

"I'll be all right. I got the gold," he patted his saddlebag. "How's Martha and the baby?"

"Doing well. Our daughter was born less than an hour ago."

"Good, because we need to leave immediately."

"What happened?"

"I confronted the two men who captured Elizabeth. It was Chet and Chester LaSalle who are always lazing around the trading post. I guess when they learned I'd married Jillian, they followed us into Tennessee and saw us with the gold. That must have been when they hatched their plan to abduct Elizabeth for the treasure. I shot one in self-defense, and when the other tried to finish me off, my uncle Welt got him. Welt said he'd handle things, but I'd like to get out of these parts as quickly as possible. Those fellas with the land lottery deed are still out there, and we need to get everyone off the land as soon as we can."

Henry nodded in agreement, a worried expression furrowing his brow.

When they arrived, Jesse instructed Henry to ready the horses and the wagon. He could hear the cries of a newborn baby as he approached the front door. Elizabeth's and Jillian's eyes lifted suddenly as Jesse strode boldly through the door. Bright crimson blood saturated the handkerchief around his upper arm and drizzled down his arm, wrist and hand.

"Jesse!" Jillian exclaimed and ran to him.

"Here's your gold," he slammed the bag down on the kitchen table dramatically. "It was Chet and Chester. They took Elizabeth. Guess they followed us up to McMinn County and saw us with the gold."

"Look what's happened to you!" She ignored his remark and immediately rushed to him and fingered the edge of the bloody bandage around his arm. "Are you hurt anywhere else?"

"No, just my arm." He looked pale and weak. "Get Martha and the baby. Henry's preparing the wagon."

"We need to take care of your arm! Elizabeth, get a knife, tweezers, and soap," Jillian ordered, and Elizabeth immediately set in search of the items.

"We have to leave, now," he barked. "Welt and I just shot two men for that gold, and the Bishop brothers are still out there aiming to collect on those land lottery deeds."

"You should never have gone after them!" Jillian's brow furrowed with worry.

"I had to do it. It was the only way I could prove to you that you can trust me."

"Jesse," her eyes filled with tears as she clung to him. "I'm so sorry! It's all my fault that you're wounded."

"We don't have time for tears or apologies. Go make a bed for Martha in the back of the wagon," he turned and left. Relieving Henry of his task, he told him to bring

Martha and the baby to the wagon. In short order they had loaded the wagon, and Jesse started to climb into the front.

"Now listen to me, Jesse Whitmore. You need that arm tended to! Henry, drive the wagon. Elizabeth, ride up front with Henry." She tugged Jesse's good arm, leading him to the rear of the wagon while Henry and Elizabeth followed orders. Jillian had made a bed for Jesse next to Martha's, and motioned for him to lie down. He did not resist for the blood loss had rendered him dizzy and fatigued.

Martha rested comfortably with the baby in the crook of her arm, the exhaustion of the birth experience inducing a relaxing sleep. Jillian knelt beside her husband and set to work on his arm. He winced as her fingers probed the wound with the wagon bumping along the dirt road. The bullet lodged inside the flesh of his bicep, and Jillian gave him a blade to bite as she extricated the metal.

After removing the bullet, she began cleansing and dressing the wound. All the while, she asked him questions about what had transpired at the burial grounds. When she had completed the painful task, she wiped her hands with a dampened handkerchief and settled beside him once more. Gently, she smoothed his hair to the side, letting her fingers linger in its softness.

"You shouldn't have done it, Jesse! It wasn't worth it."

"Is our life together worth it?" he asked, his eyes saddened. She hated herself for dimming the light that once shined in his eyes. She'd driven him too far - asked too much. Now he'd killed a man just to prove his loyalty to her. Of course, it had been self-defense, yet still Jesse had never killed before.

She leaned her head on his chest, placing her arms around his waist. "I'm so sorry, Jesse. I should have trusted you unconditionally. It was wrong of me to ever doubt you. I just kept hearing Running Deer's voice telling me that no white man could be trusted and that you were out for the treasure. Then he died in such a cruel way at the hands of those horrible men and I... I just-"

"It's all right, Jillian," he stroked her long dark hair with his hand. "I can understand why it would be hard for you to trust my kind after everything you've been through."

"But you're not like them, and I knew that all along. Why did I allow myself to entertain such doubts?" Tears spilled freely from her eyes onto his chest. He lifted her chin with his finger, gazing deeply into her cinnamon eyes.

She could read the forgiveness in his expression and felt the understanding compassion in his kiss as he took her in the strength of his embrace, pressing his lips gently to hers. As his kiss deepened, she felt the promise of eternity in Jesse's love and knew that whatever may come, he would be at her side to allay her fears and remind her that some things in life are a lot more important than gold, treasures, and land.

Several days later when the villagers' wagons rolled onto their new property, Jillian sat in the front of the wagon next to her husband, holding Martha's baby girl lovingly in her arms. Jillian released a sigh knowing that the haunted past could finally be laid to rest and the prospects of a bright new future lay on the horizon.

Epilogue

Caleb and Joshua Whitmore setup camp along the winding, rushing river. The roar of the rapids was only broken by the whippoorwill's song, and Joshua's occasional irritated grunt as he attempted to erect his tent. Exasperated, he flung a pole to the earth, clanging it on a nearby rock, and running his fingers through his auburn hair.

"Just a minute, and I'll help you with that," Caleb told his brother as he finished building a fire. Caleb swiped his hands together and then dusted them on his jeans. "Aren't you glad I took the initiative to become an Eagle Scout?" the thirty-year-old chuckled. "Don't you wish you'd done the same?"

"No, I hated Scouts. Plus, why do I need to know anything about camping when I have you around?" he patted his older brother's back soundly and stepped aside, letting Caleb finish constructing the tent.

"You do my taxes, and I'll raise your tents," Caleb chuckled at his brother, the accountant.

"After raising my tent, how about coming out to the house and fixing my broken garbage disposal while you're at it? Heather's been badgering me for weeks about that thing." Joshua put his hands on his hips and watched Caleb work.

"You still haven't fixed that thing?" Caleb rolled his eyes and shook his head. "Why don't you hire a plumber?"

"Why do I need a plumber when my brother's Mister Fixit?" Joshua laughed and stepped toward the river, gazing out over the waters, the lush green vegetation and clear blue sky. He turned his head over his shoulder, directing his voice toward Caleb, "Do you think we're close?"

"Don't know. Hope so."

"How many more waterfalls do you think there are to search?"

"There's several along here. Not really sure," Caleb shrugged.

"I hope the gold's still there after all these years - especially since I could be taking a vacation with the wife and kids at Disney World instead of roughing it out here with you all week," Joshua squatted down, letting his hands wade through the icy water.

"We've wanted to look for it since we were kids. If nothing else, after this trip we'll know whether the gold's still there, or whether Jillian and Jesse came back for it."

"Or, if someone else came along and took it. After all, they had six children, and that story's been passed down for centuries. Who's to say we're the first to come in search of it," Joshua added, and then gazed up into the lush vegetation of late summer. He thought back on the story of his ancestors, and their flight from the area nearly two hundred years earlier at just this time of year.

"Let's get dinner started. We'll turn in soon and make an early start of it in the morning. Maybe tomorrow will be our lucky day," Caleb opened his backpack and handed his brother a dehydrated meal packet.

"Why can't they dehydrate donuts in these things?" Joshua muttered.

"Find the cave, and I'll buy you a gross of donuts on our way back home!" Caleb slapped his brother's back and set to work preparing his meal.

The next morning, the brothers rose bright and early to set out in search of the cave their fourth great grandmother had seen in her youth. Family legend had passed the tale down through the generations. Whether it was accurate or a tall tale was yet to be seen, but the adventure was one the men had planned ever since their mother told them the story as youth.

Caleb's chest beat anxiously as they approached a waterfall that poured into a crystal clear blue lake. Without a word, he let his backpack ease to the earth, removed his pants and shirt and dove into the water. Joshua followed his brother, and the pair swam across the water. A picture of his grandmother standing in the falls with her betrothed nearby entered Caleb's mind, and he wondered whether the vision were simply his imagination or an echo from the past. When he reached the other side, he pulled himself atop a rock beside the waterfall and leaned over to give his brother a hand out of the water.

Each man carried a small waterproof flashlight on a chain around his neck, prepared for the dark cave they hoped to find behind the waterfall. Eagerly they hastened their pace and approached the falls, slipped behind it and found an opening. Eyes wide, they stared at each other and ventured back into the cave.

"A hundred feet, the story goes," Joshua said, as he began counting his paces.

They shined their flashlights around the cavern, but there were no gold bars, no baskets of amber nuggets or shimmering silver. Just an empty cave.

"Another dead end!" Joshua exclaimed and kicked at the dirt floor beneath his feet. "Ouch!"

"What's wrong?"

"I've gone and cut my foot on something," Joshua fussed in irritation.

"Let me see," Caleb pointed his flashlight down at his brother's upturned foot. Joshua stood holding it in his hands, hopping on one foot.

Caleb's breath caught, unable to speak.

"What? What's wrong?" Joshua asked, flashing his light in Caleb's astonished eyes and then down at his foot.

"I'm not bleeding, I don't think," Joshua muttered, examining his toes more closely.

"Not your foot. Look!"

Caleb pointed his flashlight down at the ground where Joshua had kicked up the earth. There shimmering in the dust lay a shiny gold nugget! Quickly Caleb knelt down, lifted the metal and held it up to his brother's view.

"Is that what I think it is?" Joshua gasped.

"Looks like gold to me!" Caleb exclaimed as he rubbed the metal against his teeth to test its softness.

Immediately Joshua knelt on the ground and ran his fingers through the dust. Caleb put the nugget he'd found in his pocket and joined his brother in his search.

Later that afternoon the brothers emerged from the cave, each carrying a small pouch of gold. It wasn't much. It wasn't a cave full, but it was enough to prove the story true. The villagers had evidently gone back for the gold and in their haste to remove it, missed a few nuggets here and there. Only after a thorough search with metal detectors and groping on their hands and knees had the men been able to find what remained of their ancestors' treasure.

"It won't make us millionaires," Joshua said, as he held up his share of the gold in a small leather pouch and jiggled it, "but I believe I'm more excited to know the story's true than anything else."

"Me too," Caleb agreed, tossing his arm around Joshua, patting his back. The brothers started their trek back to civilization - back to their modern life and modern freedoms — more grateful than ever for their ancestors whose love found a way to overcome insurmountable odds and bridge two very different worlds.

About the Story

Beyond the Waterfall is a blend of local and family history. The story goes that as a young woman, my quarter-Cherokee third great grandmother on my mother's side was blindfolded, taken down the river and shown a Cherokee treasure trove. She lived in the East Tennessee, Northwest Georgia area. My mother has told me the story numerous times over the years; and when I started writing historical fiction, I thought the story of Jemima Elliott would make a wonderful basis for a book. As I researched, I learned of Chief Joseph Vann who was driven from the area in 1835. Being the second wealthiest man in America at the time, my mother mused as to the possibility that it could have been his treasure that Jemima saw.

After conducting a search on the internet for "Cherokee treasure," I learned that there's a legend of Cherokee gold hidden behind a waterfall along Hwy 411. This is near Spring Place, Georgia, where Joe Vann's mansion still stands. I took a trip to the Vann House to learn as much as I could about the man and the period. So, I combined the three stories, added a twist of imagination and romance and the result is *Beyond the Waterfall*. I hope you enjoyed it! You may view pictures of my visit to the Vann house by going to www.MarniePehrson.com and clicking on the link for the tour of Chief Joseph Vann's house.

The epilogue is dedicated to my two sons, Caleb and Joshua, whose first comment upon hearing the story is always, "You think the gold's still there? Let's go get it!"

About the Author

Marnie L. Pehrson was born and raised in the Chattanooga, Tennessee area. An avid enthusiast of family history, Marnie integrates elements of the places, people and events of her Southern family and heritage into her historical fiction romances. Marnie's life is steeped in Southern history from the little town of Daisy that she grew up in, to the 24 acres bordering the famous Chickamauga Battlefield upon which her family resides. The Chickamauga Battlefield inspired her book ***Rebecca's Reveries*** and e-books, ***Back in Emily's Arms*** and *In Love We Trust*.

Marnie's background is in inspirational works such as *Lord, Are You Sure?* Her first novel, ***The Patriot Wore Petticoats***, is based on the true story of Marnie's heroic fourth great-great grandmother, Laodicea "Daring Dicey" Langston. It was Dicey's remarkable life story and the encouragement from her friend, Marcia Lynn McClure, that persuaded her to step outside her typical inspirational titles to venture into historical fiction. With Marnie's inspirational writing background, you can always count on a moral to every story.

Marnie and her husband Greg live with their six children in Ringgold, Georgia in a house that Marnie designed. You may read more of her work at www.MarniePehrson.com and www.CleanRomanceClub.com or reach her at marnie@pwgroup.com or 706-866-2295.

Other Books by Marnie Pehrson

The Patriot Wore Petticoats
Historical fiction, 224, pages, ISBN: 0-9729750-4-7
Daring "Dicey" Langston, the bold and reckless rider and expert shot, saves her family and an entire village during the American Revolution. Having faced British soldiers, rushing swollen rivers, the "Bloody Scouts," and the barrel of a loaded pistol, nothing had quite prepared this valiant heroine for the heart-pounding exhilaration she'd find in the arms of one brave Patriot. Based on a true story about the author's fourth great-grandmother. Learn more at www.DiceyLangston.com

Rebecca's Reveries
Historical Fiction, 224 pages, paperback, ISBN: 0-9729750-2-0
Rebecca Marchant had led a sheltered life until she found herself inexplicably drawn to the home of her father's youth. Surrounded by the historical landscape of the Chickamauga Battlefield in Georgia, Rebecca finds herself plagued by haunting dreams and vivid visions of Civil War events. As Rebecca walks a mile in another girl's moccasins through her visions and dreams she learns about compassion, forgiveness, temptation and the power of true love.

Hannah's Heart
Historical Fiction, 116 pages, paperback, ISBN: 0-9729750-6-3
Hannah Jamison made the mistake of falling for the wrong man. Not only did he find her irritating and troublesome, but also her father had no use for him. All seemed a hopeless infatuation until Mother Nature threw the two together in the perfect time and place. But now what to do about her father? A fictional story based on a true account of Marnie's great-grandparents.

Waltzing with the Light
Historical fiction, 268 pages, paperback, 0-9729750-5-5
Nestled within the valley of the Appalachian mountains, Daisy, Tennessee, seemed like a sleepy little town until depression-era drifter, Jake Elliot, entered it and knocked on the front door of the yellow farm house and met Mikalah, the oldest of the Ford children. Little did he know how his life and his heart would be affected from that moment forward. Although Daisy seems peaceful and inviting, for a member of the LDS faith it has its ruthless characters and dangerous moments which threaten Jake & Mikalah's plans and their very lives. The misconceptions over Jake's beliefs test the metal of everyone he encounters, bringing out the best in the most loveable characters and the worst in those with more treacherous motives.

Lord, Are You Sure?
Inspirational, 152 pages, ISBN 0-9729750-0-4
A roadmap for understanding how Heavenly Father works in your life, helping you understand why certain problems keep repeating themselves, how to break the cycle and unlock the mystery of why you encounter challenges and roadblocks on roads you felt inspired to travel.

10 Steps to Fulfilling Your Divine Destiny: A Christian Woman's Guide to Learning & Living God's Plan for Her
Inspirational, 124 pages, ISBN 0-9676162-1-2
Have you ever said to yourself, "I'd love to do great things with my life, but I'm just too busy, too untalented, too ordinary, too afraid, too anything but extraordinary"? Inside this book you'll learn how to reach your full God-given potential.

To order call 800-524-2307 or visit www.MarniePehrson.com
Also visit www.CleanRomanceClub.com

Printed in the United States
153370LV00002B/19/A